# Enjoying True Peace

Yasmin Peace Series Book 5

# Enjoying True Peace

WOODLAND HIGH SCHOOL
800 N. MOSELEY DRIVE
STOCKBRIDGE, GA 30281
(770) 389-2784

## Stephanie Perry Moore

MOODY PUBLISHERS

CHICAGO

Yasmin Peace Series Book 5

All Scripture quotations are taken from the King James Version.

Lyrics on page 156 from the song entitled "Praise Him in Advance." From the album entitled "Thirsty" by Marvin Sapp, Verity Label, July 2007.

"Better Than I," cited on page 151, lyrics by John Bucchino, in *Joseph: King of Dreams*, directed by Rob LaDuca, Robert C. Ramirez, DreamWorks, 2000.

Drug information in chapter 10 has been adapted from the Foundation for a Drug-Free World website, http://www.drugfreeworld.org/#/drugfacts.

Editor: Kathryn Hall
Interior Design: Ragont Design
Cover Design and Photography: Trevell Southhall at TS Design Studios
Author Photo: Bonnie Rebholz

Library of Congress Cataloging-in-Publication Data

Moore, Stephanie Perry.
    Enjoying true peace / Stephanie Perry Moore.
      p. cm. — (Yasmin Peace series ; bk. 5)
    Summary: When her father's decision to move the whole family sends everyone in an uproar, triplet Yasmin continues to depend on God to help her remain calm and find peace in the midst of this new storm.
    ISBN 978-0-8024-8606-6
    [1. Family life—Fiction. 2. Christian life—Fiction. 3. Moving, Household —Fiction. 4. High schools—Fiction. 5. Schools—Fiction. 6.Brothers and sisters—Fiction. 7.Triplets—Fiction. 8. African Americans—Fiction.] I. Title.
PZ7.M788125En 2010
[Fic]--dc22

                                                          2009027750


1 3 5 7 9 10 8 6 4 2

*Printed in the United States of America*

To
## Rev. Andrew J. White Sr.
*(Pastor, Zion Baptist Church, Petersburg, Va.)*

*How thankful I was to have you
as my pastor when I was Yasmin's age.
Having you guide my spiritual life
was a blessing that has carried me into adulthood.
Thank you for showing me that the only true peace
in this life is found in Christ.
May every reader understand that point and
also may God bless you as you've blessed many!*

# Contents

# Chapter 1

## Darker Days Come

*L*ife is looking brighter for the Peace family!" Dad said as we were in Orlando together, celebrating New Year's. "And it's only gonna get better 'cause y'all are movin' here!"

Wait a minute. Had he said what I thought I just heard? Don't get me wrong; Orlando is pretty and all. It has its fun attractions, like Disney World and Universal Studios, which could definitely keep us occupied in a big way. I mean, who wouldn't want to live in this hugely fun city?

It was just that I had a lot going on for me back in Jacksonville. And even though I desperately wanted my family to be together, moving to Orlando wasn't the step I wanted to take at the moment. After all, I was in high school and I had a really sweet guy back at home just waiting for me to return. Besides that, I'm cool with my girlfriends too. A move like this was not something I was looking forward to at all.

As I looked over at Mom, she was smiling so hard. But I actually thought that she would be bummed out too. She had a good job and things were getting better for her in Jacksonville. But I wasn't naïve. I knew Mom wouldn't just pick up her things and change her world on a whim. She was a strong, independent Black woman. Other than my brothers and me, Mom really had no ties to Dad anymore. They weren't married any longer and I saw no new ring on her finger. Besides, we couldn't just move in with him. Although he is our father and her ex-husband, I knew this wouldn't be God's plan. So I couldn't help but think that there was more to this story.

"So why the long faces?" Mom asked with concern as she examined the reaction she was getting from the three of us.

I hadn't even realized that York and Yancy were frowning too. I was so deep in my own gloomy thoughts that I'd never even looked over at them. But they didn't appear happy about this news either.

York called out, "We just got our basketball thing goin'." He looked like he wanted to punch the wall or something.

"Yeah, and Coach Hicks said we got a really good shot at winning state. So far, we're undefeated. Dad, why can't you just move in with us?" Yancy added.

"Plus, what's the hurry? Why are y'all movin' so fast?" York blurted out.

The questions were coming so quickly; neither of my parents had a chance to respond. At York's remark, both of them gave him a similar look like, *Boy, don't act grown on us.*

True, we weren't grown yet. We were growing teenagers in the ninth grade of high school. It was time for them to realize we weren't their little babies anymore. Having seen a lot in our fourteen years of life had helped us mature. We'd lost our older brother to suicide. We were raised while our dad had been in jail. We'd witnessed our mom struggle to put food on the table. And we had even survived an apartment fire.

And now that things were looking up, our whole world would have to suddenly change? Why were our parents moving so fast? Just a couple of weeks ago Mom didn't even want to join in on the trip to Orlando for Christmas. Exactly what was going on here? How could she have a change of heart so quickly?

"Can I say something?" York asked cautiously, making sure he wasn't gonna get hit for his last smart-aleck comment.

Dad said, "Sure, Son, go ahead. We wanna hear from you, but do know that the decision is already made. We know we got strong-willed kids, but your mom and I don't owe y'all any explanations. You gotta understand that we know what's best for you. I know that I haven't been there much throughout you guys' lives. But I do have three and a half years left to spend with you all before you go off to college."

At that statement, York gave him a bewildered glare.

Reading his son's look, Dad went on. "Yeah, York, I know you gonna get those grades together and you're gonna go on to college too, Son. 'Cause having a male authority figure around the house is gonna help keep you straight. Now, what do you have to say?"

"I've just never been a part of anything organized like the basketball team. Now that I've gotten into it, I'm pretty good at it. I may not be as good as Jeff Jr. was, but I do wanna give it a try."

Then York took a deep breath to gather his courage; he was ready to present the rest of his case. "So I wanna stay with Uncle John for a while. And, Dad, it can't be because I like him better than you or anything like that. 'Cause that's not it. You're my dog;

you know that. It's just that he lives in Jacksonville, and he's got an extra bedroom. When I watched the kids for them one night, it was cool being over there. I just think Yancy and Yasmin should move with y'all and I should stay in Jacksonville and finish school here."

Yancy quickly protested, "Yeah, but they only have one extra room, and I think that room should be mine. I have more reason to stay in Jacksonville than York or Yas. I mean, no offense, Pops, but Uncle John has always been like a dad to me. Seriously, we've been doing a lot together over the years. It was York who never really liked him."

"Wait, I like him now!" York objected.

"Yeah, okay. Right," Yancy coolly replied. "But really, folks, listen, my grades are up to par. I'm on the honors track and basketball is taking off for me too. I should be the one to stay in Jacksonville. York and Yasmin should move to Orlando with you."

Dad just listened and turned to me. "Yas, I know you have somethin' to say."

I was fuming with anger. Was it finally my turn? How dare they? My brothers just felt so sure that I needed to be the one to move. I was doing everything in my power to hold back the tears. Yes, I was happy for my parents. They were trying to work it out, trying to make us a family again. Besides, I had no doubt that they would do it God's way. That meant wedding bells would be in their plans soon enough.

But even though they hadn't told us everything, I couldn't spoil their plans by wanting things my own way. I just felt like, of all the people, I should be the one to stay in Jacksonville. It just seemed too selfish to express my true feelings, so I didn't say anything.

In my silence, Mom spoke up. "Obviously, she's fine with it since she has nothin' to say. I'm sure she's gonna miss her friends and school, but she'll be okay. That's the problem nowadays. Kids get too many choices in this world. The decision has been made and we're all gonna move. None of y'all are stayin' in Jacksonville. The plan your dad and I have is for the three kids we have left to be a family—all under one roof. And if your dad has to be in Orlando to land the job that's he's been workin' on gettin', then this is where we'll all be when that time comes." Mom flatly put it all out there; she didn't leave any room for changing her mind.

York was furious. "Wow, Mom! How you gonna just forget what we want like we ain't got no say in it? I mean, when is this move supposed to be happenin' anyway? You were the one who encouraged us to get involved in basketball in the first place. So now we've done it, and we're gettin' good at it. But you just wanna pull that away from us?"

She just shook her head and said, "You'd better watch your mouth, boy."

"I'm just sayin', Ma," York responded, trying to persuade her to see it his way.

"It's not what you say, Son. It's how you say it," Dad cut in, motioning for him to calm down.

York just grabbed his jacket and stormed out of the hotel room. I wanted to join him. And looking over at Yancy, he did too. We both knew that York had a tougher spirit, and he was bold enough to pull a move like that.

"York, you'd better get back in here!" Mom yelled.

I screamed to myself, *Run, York, run for me!*

"Let him go," Dad said. "Yancy, go and check on your brother."

Then he told Mom, "The boys need to go and cool down."

"Yeah, well, I need to cool down too," she said as she headed toward the door. Before she went out, she looked over at me. "They're gonna come around, though; they'll be okay with our decision like you are, Yasmin." She really thought that I was on board with the whole thing, and I hadn't given her any reason not to.

As she walked out leaving Dad and me alone, I couldn't help feeling extremely sad. *But, Mom, I'm not okay with this,* I silently confessed as the tears rolled down my face.

In those few minutes after she left, Dad and I didn't speak. He turned on the TV, and I went outside in the darkness. When I found my brothers sitting on a nearby bench, I sat next to them. The three of us said nothing to one another, but we all felt the same unhappiness. We just looked up at the sky. It was very clear that our world was changing and we were unable to control what was about to happen.

Three days later we had said good-bye to Dad and were back in Jacksonville. I wasn't sure when we'd see him again, so the huge hug we shared would have to last for a while.

On the day of the basketball tournament, we were at the school gymnasium. This was a big chance for my brothers and they were all geeked about it.

"It just seems so weird," Veida said to me as we sat with my other two crazy best buds. "Why your parents gonna move y'all like that? How am I gonna live without seeing your fine brothers every day?"

"Now . . . you wrong for that," Perlicia scolded her. "Neither

York or Yancy are thinkin' about you; trust me. You should be thinkin' about missin' your friend and here you are talkin' about some boys. You're a hot mess, girl."

"No, no. Yas, don't get me wrong. I'm gonna miss you. Seriously. All of this stuff I've been goin' through with my parents not gettin' along and my sister trippin', I wouldn't have been able to manage if I didn't have you to call and talk to."

Turning the attention away from herself, Veida continued. "And speaking of boys, these two chicks over here got some new love interests. They keep talkin' about it, but they won't spill the details." She motioned to Asia and Perlicia.

"What? I was only gone for a minute! What boys y'all got?" I asked in complete surprise.

"Veida doesn't know what she's talkin' about," Asia responded, dismissing my question and the subject.

My three friends looked so cute in their Trojanette outfits. Their short skirts and color-coordinated tops really made them stand out from me. I hated so badly that I didn't make the squad with them, but I was proud to see them dance during halftime. My girls knew they were the bomb. I was just glad that they still wanted to sit with me.

"So," Veida started. "Does Myrek even know yet?" She scooted closer to get the scoop.

Her question made me get emotional again. Myrek wasn't just another boyfriend. We'd been friends for years. And every time either one of us wanted to break up, our friendship drew us back together again. How could I tell him that I had to move?

There was still no set date as to when we were leaving. And I didn't want breaking the news to him to make him doubt my feelings. So I hadn't told him yet because I was afraid of how he would react. Besides, if he was gonna be okay with us having a long-distance relationship, then I would be mad. 'Cause if that was the case, then he really didn't care as much as I thought he did. Just thinking about it all was too hard to bear. It seemed like I couldn't win either way.

"I just hope they don't move y'all before we go to state because these boys are on the case!" Veida said, jumping to her feet when Myrek made a basket.

"Well, they ain't so on-point right now," Asia added. "Look at the score. We're goin' into halftime with us twenty points down."

"Hey, Yas. There's your mom," Veida said. I looked up in surprise and saw my mother headed to a seat two sections down.

In fact, I was really shocked. What was she doing here? She was supposed to be at work until 6 p.m., so Myrek's dad was going to take us home. Seeing her show up for the game, even though my brothers would be excited about it, made me hope everything was okay.

*This is strange,* I thought. "I'll be back, y'all," I said to them as I got up.

"Well, we gotta go and get ready for the fourth-quarter short dance. We'll see you when we get back," Veida said.

"She knows we're gettin' ready to perform. You don't have to rub it in," Perlicia reprimanded.

Veida shot back. "I know she knows. I was just remindin' her that we should be here by the time she comes back. Back off, Perlicia!"

"It's okay, girls. Go out there and do your thing," I told them.

As I headed over to see my mom, the three of them went to join the other dancers. I had to keep my own feelings in check so that the green-eyed monster wouldn't pop up and step into my business. I was happy for my girls; we were true friends. I only hoped when I moved to Orlando that I would have friends just as caring. It took a lot for us to become tight buddies. Now I truly believed that we wouldn't intentionally deceive each other—and that just felt so great.

Even so, I couldn't help but wonder. Would it be possible to have meaningful friendships with some new girls? Or have I found something that I would never be able to replace? Then again, how could my parents do this to me? I never had good girlfriends until now, and they knew that. It made me angrier with each step I took toward my mom.

When I approached her, I just blurted out, "Why aren't you at work?" It sounded so cold even to me. I just couldn't keep my feelings in.

"Because I'm here. And watch your tone!" she snapped back. "Look, Yasmin, I know you've been avoiding me. You've been stayin' in your room, having your head stuck in some book, or talkin' on the phone with your little friends. But we need to talk about this. Your dad and I are tryin' not to move until the end of the semester, but we may have to move sooner. It all depends on what happens with this job he's tryin' to get. Life changes and you might not like it, but you've gotta be able to roll with it and adjust to survive."

"All right, Mom." I said whatever I could just so she could stop talking about the move. Right now the attention needed to be on my brothers' game.

"Look at 'em," she said with a frustrated tone. "Your brothers are gettin' beat down bad. Pick up the game, boy!" she yelled out. "York, get the rebound! Hey, Coach, you need to get Yancy up off the bench and maybe y'all would do better!" she shouted.

"Mom!" I said, feeling embarrassed and wanting her to calm down.

"I'm just tellin' the truth."

When the game was over, our team didn't win. Myrek and my brothers were really upset. Mom went to my brothers and tried to give them pointers. But neither of them wanted to hear it. It's like she was mad at all of us for being mad about moving. And her over-the-top frustration was getting the best of her.

When he didn't come up to me, I went over to Myrek. Trying to cheer him up, I said, "It's okay. You'll get 'em next time."

"Yeah, but will you even be here to see it?"

I couldn't believe this! One of my brothers, I didn't know which one, had opened his big mouth. We all agreed that I'd be the one to tell Myrek about us moving.

All I could say to him was, "I didn't wanna talk about it, Myrek. I didn't wanna bring it up because it makes me mad. I don't wanna move. Okay? And no matter what you say about the situation, it's gonna hurt my feelings."

"I don't understand. What do you mean?" Myrek asked me, wiping the sweat from his brow.

I tried to explain the way I felt. "If you tell me you'll miss me, then I'll be sad. If you tell me that it's gonna be okay because life goes on and we're too young to have anything serious anyway, then I'm gonna be bummed out too. Nothin' you say is gonna make me feel better about this move."

Then he grabbed my hand, and I saw his eyes beginning to tear up. "I don't need to *say* anything. Can't you tell by my face how I feel about you movin' away?"

As a tear, mixed with the sweat already on his face, dropped from his eye, I knew that he was bummed out too. I'm sure some of it had to do with them losing the game and with him missing some free throws. But why in the world did I have to have such bad news?

*Lord,* I thought, *please fix this. I can't stand anything else clobbering my world down.*

⌘

I was so glad when classes finally started. I needed to get away from all the tension that was going on in my home. Mom was into planning her future, so she was preoccupied. There were boxes all around the apartment as we prepared to move. My brothers were tied up with their basketball practice and actually getting along for a change. They didn't have time to hang out with me. So, for the most part, I was left alone with my thoughts. But I knew school would keep me occupied until it was time for me to leave.

I had just left the counselor's office after getting my new schedule when I bumped into someone. I looked up and couldn't help but stare. This new guy was cute. We just laughed at our slight collision.

"I'm sorry. I'm so clumsy," he said in the most polite manner I've ever seen on a ninth-grade boy.

I could see the developing muscles poking from under his sweater. But I had to stop staring before people reported back to Myrek that I was looking at this kid a little too hard.

"So, you're new here, huh?" I asked. "I haven't seen you around before."

"Yeah, I'm the new kid on the block."

"Where did you come from?" I asked.

"Pensacola. This school is a lot bigger than my old one. I'm tryin' not to get lost."

I replied, "Let me see your schedule. I'm just a freshman but I know my way around."

"I'm a freshman too," he said.

But I knew that already by how young he looked. I asked him where he lived. It couldn't be too far from me since we attended the same school. When he said the name of his apartment complex, I sort of laughed.

"What's wrong?" He went on, "I mean, I know I don't live in the nicest area, but please fill me in. What goes on around there? Are we gonna be robbed left and right? What? Talk to me."

I explained. "Yeah, well, I live in the neighborhood next to yours. You know how it is—kids not liking each other because they live on opposite sides of the street."

"I mean, I'm not in any gang or anything like that. Plus, I don't like being around trouble," he told me.

This guy was pretty smooth and I like how he complimented my style. I kept telling myself, *You have a boyfriend!* But there was nothin' wrong with me being friends with him, right? I just showed him around and he was so appreciative.

"You don't have to thank me anymore," I said to him after he must have thanked me a dozen times.

"Yes, I do. It's not easy being the new kid. But if everyone here is as nice as you are, then I'm gonna like it here."

Before I could get his name, Asia and Perlicia came up on both sides of me, put their arms in mine, and tugged me away. "Y'all, I was talkin'. Don't be rude."

"Well, it looks like you're gettin' too close to me, all caught up, or whatever. Don't you know if Myrek walked down this hall right now he would be furious?" Asia whispered in my ear.

"He's a new student and I'm tryin' to show him the way around. We're just doing what friends do." I didn't want to sound too defensive.

"You just met him. How could y'all possibly be friends?" Perlicia said, rolling her eyes.

"Whatever. You two are being silly."

The day flew right past me. At lunchtime my girls were nowhere to be found and it looked like we had different lunch periods. I was so bummed out. Who was I gonna talk to? Who was I gonna hang with? And then it dawned on me that I could chill with my new friend. Funny, I didn't even know his name. But just then I saw him across the room.

Actually, I heard him too because he was sort of being loud. I didn't realize right away that he was saying some bogus things to the folks around him. Thinking he would recognize me from earlier, I just went up to him and smiled.

"What you lookin' at?" he asked in a harsh tone.

It sounded strange and I didn't know how to respond because it seemed like he meant it. I couldn't walk away because he was standing right in front of me. People had started laughing and none of this felt good.

"I said, what you lookin' at? I don't know you," he snarled.

How could he play me like that? Earlier I had shown him to his class and gave him a preview of the school. He was cool then and over-the-top nice. What had gone on in a matter of hours?

But I wasn't about to hold back. "Don't act like you don't know me. If you don't wanna be friends, that's all you have to say. I just came over here to see if you wanted to eat lunch with me."

"Whoa! Pensacola ain't got nothin' on y'all Jacksonville girls. Y'all are straight. What, you gonna buy my lunch too?" he said while sliding closer to me in a sleazy kind of way.

Tugging away, I said, "Please, just back up off of me!"

"What's going on?" Myrek asked. He came over to us with concern all over his face.

"I'm tryin' to get my rap on. Why is it any of yo' business?" The guy I had sorely misjudged was saying this to my boyfriend.

Myrek immediately got tough. "You don't need to get your rap on with her. Just step off so we won't have no trouble."

"Myrek, it's okay. Let's just go," I said, pulling my guy back.

"No, no. Bring your man back over here. Tell him how you were all over me, askin' me to eat lunch with you."

Myrek looked at me. "What? What is he talkin' about?"

I was so humiliated! I felt like I'd been punked. Why couldn't I just be satisfied with my own boyfriend? No, I had to be lured in by some charm and a smile. Now look where it got me. Myrek and I had been in a great place in our relationship. He trusted me and I trusted him. But I had gone and messed it all up.

It felt like the sun had suddenly gone away and grey clouds had taken its place. I knew that I had disappointed Myrek. He just walked away, shaking his head. The guy was rude and spiteful; he just stood there laughing in my face.

I ran straight to the girls' restroom and cried. With my head against the stall, I prayed, *Lord, why do things have to be so down for me? Why do only darker days come?*

# Chapter 2

## Holder of Pain

*W*ait, Myrek, please, let me explain!" I called out. Lunch period hadn't ended yet, but I had taken a few minutes to dry my eyes and pull myself together. When I stepped into the hallway, he was just leaving the cafeteria after that embarrassing scene. Ignoring me, he headed down the hallway. It didn't take long for me to realize that he didn't want to talk to me.

When I caught up with him, he hurt my feelings even more. "What, Yas, what do you want? I'm tryin' to go to class. Go on and leave me alone!"

"Can't we just talk? I want to explain," I pleaded.

"I ain't tryin' to hear it. That new dude told me everything I needed to know. You're not happy with us?"

"That's not it at all. Seriously, Myrek."

Just as he was about to walk away, the first bell rang. Myrek raised his voice to speak over the loud noise, "We'll talk about all

this later. You're movin' anyway. Maybe I'm the one takin' this relationship thing too deep."

Myrek walked down the hall as Veida came up beside me and
asked, "What's going on with you and Myrek?"

"Why does somethin' have to be going on with us?"

"You know that brother never rushes to get away from you.
Now he's shoutin' at you in the hallway. And that look on his face
seems like real trouble."

I sighed and followed her over to the lockers. I just laid my
head on hers. Unfortunately, she was mostly right about what she
had just witnessed.

"Don't worry about it. You break up with him and there are
plenty more fish in the sea. Ooh, speaking of new fish. Girl, there's
this new guy in my class. He is so cute and so nice," Veida gushed.

"Been there, done that. Please talk about somethin' else," I
urged as I stood up straight.

"No, you ain't seen this boy yet because, if you had, you
wouldn't be wantin' to change the subject so quickly. Maybe that's
what Myrek's problem is. He needs to see that you are too cute and
you don't have to wait around on him. If he's actin' crazy, you can
get somebody else. And just maybe I need to make your brothers
turn their heads toward me again."

What was this girl talking about? "What has this got to do
with my brothers, Veida? And how could that help me?" I asked
her in frustration. I just wanted to be real and have her be honest
with me too. "You said you messed up by liking both of them, but
for the last week or two you been talkin' about both of them again.
I thought it was Yancy you were all excited over. What is up with
you?"

"It was, until York got me a little somethin' for Christmas," she said with a silly smile on her face.

"What?" I asked her with surprise in my voice. This was the first time I'd heard about any of that.

"Remember when we sent out those candy cane grams before the holidays?" She reminded me of that fun project.

"You mean those little fifty-cent messages? That's what you're talkin' about? Please . . . he sent out a ton of those things."

"I doubt it," she replied. She totally didn't want to believe me.

"And I don't know; he's got it goin' on now. He's not being so abrasive anymore, and he's hangin' with the right crowd. You know, my heart broke with everything that happened to Bone. I learned my lesson; I'm not going to go back and forth. I'm just sayin' maybe I need your help to get York jealous." Veida was rambling and making no sense.

"Speaking of the guilty," I said as I saw both my brothers coming down the hall with Perlicia and Asia. They were all laughing and having fun.

Veida started primping. She couldn't even tell that my brothers weren't giving her any attention. They were so into being silly and having fun—chasing girls seemed to be the last thing on their minds. But that didn't stop Asia and Perlicia from hanging on to their every word; they couldn't stop laughing.

I finally asked them, "What is so funny? What do my brothers have y'all all giddy about?"

"They're hilarious; you know your brothers," Perlicia commented.

"The new boy thought he had game," Asia spilled and told.

"Your brothers just got him in check, so he won't be messin' with you no more," Perlicia explained as my brothers strolled away without saying a word to me.

"Why would they go off on the new guy?" Veida asked. "He's so nice, shy almost."

"No, he ain't. He's a loudmouth jerk," Asia said, looking at Veida like she'd totally misjudged the boy.

All of a sudden, the new guy walked over and started acting nice again. Who did he think he was? If it were up to me, I would tell his parents to get him the serious help this kid needed.

"Hey, I didn't catch your name earlier," he said, sounding all sweet.

"That's because I didn't give it to you," I replied as mean as I could.

Then he had the nerve to say, "I'm sorry, did I do something wrong?"

"Yeah, you did something wrong," Perlicia said as she stepped up in his face. "Havin' your hands all over me and dissin' my girl in the cafeteria is totally bogus."

"Girls, girls, I think you got the wrong one," Veida interrupted.

She just kept saying it until finally we turned around. Both Perlicia and I were stunned to see the identical face in a very similar body; even their denim shirts were similar. There were two of them? Twins!

We were all surprised at this news and the mystery was solved. The two of them were standing there together, looking so much alike, but as different as night and day. One of them was nice and kind and the other was just the opposite. The one who was hard and ghetto-acting said to the other, "The ladies are mad at you because of me." Then he turned on us and said, "I see none of y'all got your little men around, the little sissy wimps."

"Lee, get on out of here, man," one brother said to the other. Then he turned to me and said, "I should have known he was the reason you were being so weird to me. You thought I was him." Obviously, the one I met earlier was speaking to me.

Some other guys came around talking loud and being playful. I saw Lee pull one of them away, saying something crazy to the boy.

I was so embarrassed! After bashing such a sweet guy, I find out he has an evil twin! "Why didn't you tell me you had a twin?" I asked.

"I mean, the bell rang. We had to go to class. I didn't even have time to tell you my name. I'm Billy. And I apologize if my brother was rude to you. By the way, I don't know where my last class is; I was hoping you could show me."

I told my girls I would catch up with them later and the two of us started walking down the hall. Suddenly, Myrek came out of his class. I guess he left something in his locker. He walked right into us.

"You done with him, huh?" Myrek said to me, huffing and puffing.

"No, no. This is Billy, he' the guy I met earlier today. The dude at lunch is his twin brother. I'm tryin' to tell you they are two entirely different people. Now it all makes sense; one is so mean and nowhere near as cool as this guy right here," I said, pointing to Billy.

Myrek wasn't interested in my explanation. He grunted, "So you playin' hostess now? You look mighty comfortable walkin' down the hall with this dude."

"Oh, it's nothin' like that. She's just showing me to my class," Billy said as he held out his hand.

Myrek didn't shake it. "She can show you wherever, homey. Mean twin, nice twin, I'm done."

He slammed his locker shut, rolled his eyes at me, and left. I knew he was mad, but I was actually glad that I hadn't misjudged the cool boy I met earlier in the day after all. Twins! Wow. They couldn't be any more different.

"Sorry," Billy said to me. "I can see you really care about him."

We walked a little further, and I motioned to him that we had approached his classroom. "I do care about him; we've been friends forever. Hopefully, he'll calm down soon. Myrek's real levelheaded. Well, see you around school," I said and kept walking. I had to pick up the pace, class was getting ready to begin and the final bell was about to ring.

Myrek had never rolled his eyes at me. The more I thought about it the more I knew he was hurting. Actually, if we broke up I'd be hurting too. I turned the corner and hurried to my class. I couldn't help but wonder how God could make us whole again— now that my great relationship had been crushed.

On the way home from school I was still thinking about how Myrek and me could patch things up. I needed to be alone with my thoughts so I took the long route home from the school bus.

I didn't even make it around the corner before I heard a lot of loud talking and familiar voices. It sounded like my brothers and my girls. After cutting up in school earlier, what were they up to now?

Then I heard Perlicia say, "Stop, York! I already gave you one kiss. I'm not givin' you another one." Wait a minute; was she flirting with my brother?

Then Asia said to Yancy, "Let's give them some privacy."

Before I could confirm what my mind thought was going on, Myrek and I met up with each other. He must have already forgiven me because he called out in a friendly voice and said, "Yas! I was thinking about you. Looks like we're having a party! Come here, give me a hug."

"I'm stressed right now, okay? I don't know what's happening to us and it's starting to make me crazy." Having said that, I pushed past him and kept walking.

After realizing he couldn't prevent what was about to happen, he called after me, "Hey, I've got some news for you. There's something I think you should know. Your brothers have been out here entertaining your friends."

When my boyfriend blurted that out, he saw the way I was looking. I wasn't happy with that news at all. The last time my brothers got involved with one of my friends it was horrible. It was hard to believe that Perlicia and Asia would be talking to York and Yancy and didn't even share any of that with me.

I dashed around the corner and was shocked to see Perlicia and York hugged up by Myrek's dad's car. Yancy and Asia were kissing. The sight of them stopped me dead in my tracks.

"What are y'all doing!" I yelled to the top of my lungs as I saw my best friends huddled up with my brothers.

The two couples quickly pulled apart. As my whole body filled with anger, I knew this was so wrong on so many levels. Seeing my girlfriends betray their friend by being with my brothers, I wondered if I hadn't come along how far this would've gone. Even though we were ninth graders and thought we were practically grown—we weren't.

Myrek pulled at my arm; he wasn't exactly thrilled with my reaction to this situation. "You need to stay out of people's business."

"Yeah, and take my sister somewhere, man. She's ruinin' the party," York added.

Yancy said, "Yeah, Yas. Your girls don't need your permission. We got 'em."

I dismissed all three of them and turned my attention to my friends. "Asia, Perlicia, I wanna see y'all now!"

"Your brothers just told you we're straight," Asia said.

"Yeah, girl," Perlicia called out with her hands on her hips. "We only got thirty minutes before we have to be at Asia's house. Can we just have a little fun, please?"

She moved in closer and kissed York on the cheek. Asia took her cue from Perlicia and went back to cuddling up with Yancy.

I had so many questions. What about me? And what would Veida think? What about what these girls really deserved? What about what God wants? I'm supposed to be my brothers' keeper and my business was their business.

Then to make matters worse, I could look in Myrek's eyes and tell that he didn't have a problem with any of this. This was definitely a problem for me.

York wouldn't give up. "Myrek, man, handle my sister before she gets her feelings hurt," he called out.

"Come on, I wanna talk to you anyway. I just wanna hang out with my girlfriend. And I wanna apologize for being a jealous jerk.

Why are you so into stopping them instead of worrying about your own relationship?"

"This isn't about us right now, Myrek," I turned to him and said. "I'm not cool with this. And it doesn't mean that I don't want to hang out with you."

Myrek's answer surprised me. "And it doesn't mean that your brothers need you all in their business."

When he said that, it made me think really hard. Yes, I was trying to look out for my brothers, but I knew how much they cared about me too. And although they didn't want me to stop their game, how would they like it if I started mine up? I wanted them to think about it too, so I turned my back to them and started play-acting.

I wrapped my arms around Myrek and said, "Okay, Myrek, you're right. Let's have some fun. Give me a kiss!" I was trying to be as convincing as I could.

Myrek, of course, was willing to go along with me. And, just as I thought, it wasn't long before Yancy and York came running and pulled the two of us apart.

"What are y'all doin' over here?" York said to us.

Myrek couldn't even get a word in edgewise. York let him have it first. "Man, that's my sister. You can't do that with her!"

Yancy let my boyfriend know how upset it made him too. "Yeah, man. What's up with you? What you tryin' to do?"

I was right! It was like they had a double standard. What was okay for them was not okay for me. I looked over at my two girlfriends. I wanted Asia and Perlicia to understand why my brothers were against me and my boyfriend doing exactly the same thing that they were doing with York and Yancy. They didn't seem to get it, but now was not the time for them to go all the way with any boys.

As the three guys stood there arguing, I pulled my girlfriends over by a tree. They needed to come to their senses quick!

"Do y'all see how stupid it is to give it up to my brothers? Don't you see that in the back of their heads they don't think it's cool? Don't you think they should treat their girls like they want their own sister to be treated? Or do you think that they should be doggish and take what they want when it's being served to them on a silver platter? Doesn't it make sense for them to step back and do what's best for y'all?"

"Oh, Yasmin, you just need to get with it," Perlicia complained. "We're not hurtin' anybody; we're just havin' a little fun."

"Yeah," said Asia. "Just because you can't handle it doesn't mean we can't. People do mature at different stages in their lives."

"Mature? There's a baby in my family right now. You know; the one Myrek's sister had with my brother when they were in high school. Jada can't even take care of her own baby. Since she wasn't ready for the responsibility, that little girl now belongs to somebody else. You've got to be kiddin' me, Asia. There's nothin' mature about what y'all are tryin' to do."

Maybe it was wrong for me to feel betrayed, but that's how I felt. Why do my girls think this is acceptable? Why are they choosing to be with my brothers over the friendship we have? And adding to the mix how Veida feels about my brothers—everything about this arrangement was wrong. And it hurt.

Something in my communication with people wasn't right because it seemed like the folks that I thought I could trust—I couldn't. And the hurtful things people thought they could do to me were wrong too. I was going to tell my girls *and* my brothers what I thought. I was going to let them have a piece of my mind.

Myrek looked so disappointed in me. I could tell he was crushed that I wasn't trying to cuddle up with him like that. But we had a different kind of relationship and he knew it. Even though I cared about him so much, I just didn't want it to be physical. I knew me and him would have a lot to talk about later on.

He was going to have to understand that I didn't care about what anybody else did. Our relationship was going to please God. He also needed to know that he couldn't be mad at me one day and overly nice the next. I was tired of being hurt; I was tired of being left out. No more was I going to be a holder of pain.

# Chapter 3

# Disrupter
## Never Prevails

It was Friday night and my brothers had another basketball game. Since I wasn't on the dance team and it was an away game, I didn't go.

Fortunately for me, I did have something to do. Because they now had three kids, Uncle John and Aunt Lucinda hadn't spent any time alone in a while. So I volunteered to babysit and give them a chance to go out and enjoy themselves. Plus, I needed the extra money since Valentine's Day would be coming up soon and I wanted to be able to buy some gifts.

Mom was going to hang out with her girlfriend for the evening. And I was actually happy about it because she'd been so irritable lately. As much as I tried to figure out why, it was hard to tell. Before she left, she told me to take the kids in before dark. She gave me strict instructions and made it very clear not to let anyone in the house.

It had been a while since I'd seen the kids. I missed the little girl, Randi, and her little brother, Dante. When they stayed next door to us, I would watch them sometimes for their mother, Miss Sandra. My niece, Angel, was growing bigger and I had missed her too. She was already asleep in my arms so I quickly went inside and tucked her in.

Trying to keep up with the two bigger kids was no easy task; they were all over the place, playing and having fun.

"Come on, let's get ready. It's time to go inside," I told them.

"Can we play hide-and-seek again?" little Dante asked.

"It's starting to get dark," I said to him, but he kept pleading and so did his older sister. My hope was if they ran around outside for a minute or two longer they would settle down and be ready for bed. Then I'd be able to chill.

I said, "Okay, you can play one more game and then that's it. We have to go and check on Angel."

I closed my eyes and slowly counted to two. When I looked up on three, Miss Sandra was standing in front of me.

"I want to see my kids right now, Yasmin." She looked around and asked in a demanding voice, "Where are they?"

I really didn't know what to do because Mom had said no company and we were about to go inside.

Then her tone suddenly changed. In a sad and pleading voice, she said, "I just want to spend some time with my kids, Yasmin, just for a little while. Okay, please?"

"How'd you know they were here?" I said.

"I got my ways. People around here still know I miss my babies." She started to call out, "Mama's here. Mama's here."

Just the familiar sound of her voice caused the two little people to come running up to her and hug her tight around her knees.

Clearly they missed their mother. Who was I to keep them apart from each other? Technically, she was their mother and my aunt and uncle were their foster parents.

The kids started telling their mother about all the fun things they'd been doing. And I could tell from her teary eyes that she wasn't excited about being separated from them.

I couldn't help but feel sorry for her. I guess she wished she had been the one sharing in the fun they were talking about. When they ran around the yard skipping and being happy, she admitted some personal info to me.

"I'm tryin' to get myself together so I can take my babies back. I'm supposed to be givin' them what they need," she said, confirming what I suspected she was thinking.

"But at least they're safe and happy," I suggested to her.

"Yeah, but can't you see how much they miss me? I just need to spend a little more time with them. It would really bless me ... wait a minute ... I hear crying. Go ahead and see about the baby. I'll run around with them out here," Miss Sandra said.

I didn't really hear anything, but the baby had been asleep for a while. So checking on her only made good sense. Still, I didn't move right away; I was trying to think this through. When she had said it would be a blessing for her to be with the kids, I was beginning to feel the pressure.

Miss Sandra picked up on my hesitation. "You lookin' like you don't trust me or somethin'. I ain't got no car. I'm stayin' with a friend around the corner. Go ahead; I'm fine. I just want to be with the babies. I'll be right here. Go check and come back out. What if she fell out of the crib?"

I called her two kids over to me, and I asked them if they

wanted to hang out with their mom. Her son started jumping up and down. Randi was smiling wider than if she was eating cotton candy.

Dante said, "Yes, I want to play with Mommy. Please, let me play with Mommy."

Randi looked at her mom as if to say, *Where have you been? I missed you, Mommy.*

It was only going to take me a second to go in and make sure Angel was okay and then come back out. I knew I couldn't invite Miss Sandra in and the kids wanted to play a little longer. So what was the harm? I finally went in and saw that the baby was still asleep. But I noticed that she had messed up her pajamas. So I needed to change her clothes and her diaper too. She stirred a bit, but as soon as I was done, she drifted back off to sleep.

When I came back out, I thought they were still playing hide-and-seek because I didn't see Miss Sandra or the kids. But when I didn't hear any counting or giggling, I was the one making the noise. I called out to them, but I heard nothing!

Of course I panicked and immediately felt sick to my stomach. I checked the side and the front of the apartment. I stood in the middle of the sidewalk and looked up and down the street, but I couldn't find them anywhere. Had Miss Sandra played me? Had I played myself? She asked me if I trusted her and I knew that the answer was really no.

After all, this was the lady who would leave her kids at home for hours while she went out doing who knows what. When we lived next door to her, the kids would come to our house for food. She was known to say one thing and do another. All of a sudden, I knew everything I was responsible for was completely messed up.

I went back inside and got down on my knees. I prayed, *Lord, please let me find these kids. Please let them just be playing the game. Please let this not be real. Uncle John and Aunt Lucinda are responsible for the children and if something happens to them, I don't know what I'm going to do. Help!*

⟨≈⟩

I was so scared. But I got up off my knees because I knew God heard me and that gave me strength. Still, how in the world was I going to find Miss Sandra and the kids? I couldn't go and look for them. I mean, the baby was sleeping and I couldn't leave her alone. I clutched my chest because it was starting to burn.

Hoping they had come back, I opened up the door and called out their names again. Maybe they had just walked around the corner or something. But the longer I waited, the more I realized that Miss Sandra had taken them off somewhere.

I thought it would be okay to trust her, but she had told me a fib. Just because I believed she should spend a few minutes with her kids, she took advantage of the situation. Now I only hoped that I could fix it.

I had to keep believing that everything was going to be okay with the kids. Taking deep breaths, I tried to come up with a plan. That's when I thought about calling Jada; she could help me.

When she answered the phone, I quickly said, "Oh, please, you gotta help me! Please, you gotta come here now! I'm so in trouble, Jada!"

"Calm down, Yasmin. What's goin' on, girl?" Jada asked.

But I couldn't keep my excitement down. "It's the baby," I yelled. "I need you . . . help me!"

"What do you mean, it's the baby?" she said in a frantic tone.

"No, no, the baby's fine. The baby is here. But I can't go look for the other kids because I can't leave the baby, and I need your help! Quick! Come over to my house, please!"

"I don't understand what you're talking about, Yasmin. You've got to explain it to me."

"I don't have time to explain it to you!" I shouted. "Please get here, Jada. I messed up, okay?"

"All right. I'll be right over."

It wasn't even five minutes and she was walking up to my door. I had the door opened and yelled, "Hurry, please. I got to go!"

"No, you aren't goin' anywhere until you tell me what's goin' on."

"Okay, here's the quick version," I said. "I was babysitting all three of the kids for Uncle John and Aunt Lucinda."

"Okay. Where are the other two?"

"That's what I'm sayin'. They're gone."

"What do you mean, they're gone?"

I tried to explain. "Well, I was changing the baby . . ."

"You can't just leave them by themselves, you know. The oldest one can unlock the door. Did they go outside alone? You didn't tell them not to?"

"No, we were playing outside."

"And you left them outside?"

"No, no, what I'm saying is—and I know it was dumb so I don't even need you to fuss at me—I just need you to help me by watching the baby. Their mom, their real mom, came over here while we were outside. And when I came inside to check on the baby, she took her two kids and left."

Then Jada pushed me out the door. "Okay, you're right. I don't need to school you. You just need to go and try to find her."

"She wasn't driving. She said she was staying with a friend up the street. I think I know the lady she's talkin' about. I'm goin' up that way to look for them."

"My dad was driving up with your brothers and Myrek when I was leaving. They were just outside my house a few minutes ago, so maybe they saw something. What am I supposed to say if your mom or uncle comes back?"

Dropping my head, I said, "I'm so in trouble."

"You just got to tell them the truth about what happened."

"I can't believe I did this. Those kids better be okay."

"I'm sure she loves her kids and nothin' is gonna happen to them."

"Thanks, Jada, thanks."

I ran up the street. Track was coming in handy. Coach Hicks had me building my stamina up so running long distance more than forty yards was no problem.

All I could think of was those babies and how sorry I was that I'd let Miss Sandra trick me into letting her take them away.

As I approached Jada's apartment, I saw my brothers and Myrek standing outside. I screamed out, "Oh, my goodness! York, Yancy, the babies! The babies are missing!"

They heard my scream and came running to find out what was happening. "What's wrong, Yas?" York and Yancy asked in unison.

"Y'all gotta help me! It's Miss Sandra's kids—they're gone! I was babysitting them and I don't know where they are! She must have taken them!" I exclaimed.

"What do you mean; you don't know where they are?" York asked.

By now I was totally distressed, but I tried to explain.

"She tricked me. I went in to check on the baby. When I came back she was gone."

"You let her around those kids?" Yancy said. "You know she's crazy."

"Can we just pause all of this right now? We need to find those kids!"

Trying to encourage me, Myrek offered, "Maybe they're back home by now." He could see how upset I was.

"We'll go lookin'. Come on, Yancy. Myrek, let's go. Yas, does Mom know about this? Have you called Uncle John?" His questions made sense, but I couldn't give him a good answer. I was so busy tryin' to find Randi and Dante that I hadn't even stopped to think about calling anybody but Jada.

Even though I didn't say a word, York could tell from my reaction that the answer to his questions was negative. "You'd better go on back home and check things out there. If Ma's not home by now, she'll be comin' in soon. Uncle John and Aunt Lucinda are probably on their way too. Call Mom's friend's number and see if you can reach her," my brother said as he took charge of the situation.

I felt a little bit of relief at that moment. At least I was getting some help.

Then Yancy tried to console me. "Don't worry, Yas, they can't have gone too far. We'll find them," he said.

❦

I dashed back home, praying all the way. I would be so disappointed if the kids hadn't turned up yet, but my heart dropped even further when I saw Mom pulling up in the driveway. Not wanting to meet up with her, I immediately slowed down. When she saw me, she had a look on her face as if to be saying, *What are you doing out here? You're supposed to be babysitting and you're out running in the streets.* Even in the darkness, I could tell she was upset.

Mom called out, "Come here, Yasmin! You know you ain't supposed to be outside after dark!"

"Mom!" I cried.

"Don't 'mom' me! Where are your brothers? Are they back from the game yet?"

I was torn. If I told her that they were back from the game, then she would probably assume that I had sneaked away to be with Myrek. I didn't want to tell her that I was out looking for the kids because I was still hoping they were safely inside. I wanted to be free from all this drama. But I just couldn't win.

"I asked you a question, girl. Are your brothers back or not?"

"Mom, I just need to go inside really quick." I dashed past her and banged on the door extremely hard. That was a bad move in front of my mother.

"What's goin' on, Yasmin? You left those kids in there by themselves? See, you told me you needed extra money but you're not even responsible enough to handle watching children. What's the problem? Did you get into some kind of trouble?"

She kept asking me questions and I kept trying to ignore them, but I knew that was risky business. I just wanted to see those kids when Jada opened the door. "Open up! Open up!" I called out. "Jada, please open up."

"I'm comin'," Jada said.

Mom asked me, "Wait, what's Jada doin' in there?"

"Hi, Ms. Peace," Jada said when she finally opened the door.

"Where are the kids?" Mom asked, sounding really upset.

I looked at Jada. I just wanted her to say that everybody was in there, all cozy and warm. But she didn't say that. She looked away and said, "The baby's back there asleep."

"And where are the other two?" Mom questioned her as she glanced around the apartment, looking for Randi and Dante.

"Mom, it's all my fault," I said as tears burst from my eyes.

She yelled out, "Don't give me no sob story!" Then she really let me have it. "You wanted to go down there and see some little boy. Did you leave the kids? Where are they? Get to explainin', girl, and wipe those tears from your eyes. Of course this is your fault! You're big enough to go out and act grown hangin' with some boy, so be grown enough to accept your consequences. Tell me what happened! Now!"

"Ms. Peace, she didn't go down there to see my brother," Jada interrupted.

"Well, who then? Is it another boy? And you don't want Jada to know because she's gonna tell her brother?"

"Mom! I'm not like that. I'm going through something different than what you think."

"Well, if you don't tell me what happened and what's going on, then my mind can only assume the worst. The kids ain't here and you still haven't told me where they are. Did your uncle already come and get them? Why did he leave the baby?"

"I was playin' with the kids, and Miss Sandra came over—"

"What? Sandra? I thought she was out of town," Mom said, looking confused. "You didn't let her in, did you? I told you not to let anybody in under any circumstances. See, if you would just listen to what I say, you wouldn't have so many problems. Why did you let her in? Did she have alcohol on her breath? Did she threaten you?"

"No, Mom, she seemed fine. We were outside playing hide-and-seek. The kids were so happy to see her. She told me that I was a blessing to let her get a chance to hug them. At first we were all together and then the baby cried. Miss Sandra told me to go ahead and check on Angel. I never let her in. I came inside for a minute, and when I went back out, she and the kids were gone."

I couldn't stop crying as I kept telling her the whole story. "I looked all around for them. At first, I thought they were playing hide-and-seek and that's why I didn't see them. But I called for them and no one answered. When they never came back, I phoned Jada and asked her to watch the baby so I could go out and look for them. Miss Sandra said she was stayin' with a friend around the corner and she didn't have a car."

"Well, where are your brothers?"

"They're out looking for the kids now. They told me to come on back home and see about things here. I was hoping the kids were back by now, Mom. I didn't know what else to do."

"Why didn't you call me as soon as it happened?"

"On what, Mom? You don't have a cell phone anymore."

"My friend's number is on the fridge," she said, reminding me.

"I've been so upset; I wasn't thinking. I'm so sorry, Mom."

Suddenly, she changed her tone and sounded regretful. "Yeah, I need to bring more money into this house. If I had more money you wouldn't need to be tryin' to earn any. But if you're gonna work, you have to be responsible and make wise choices. Money doesn't grow on trees, you know. These days, it's hard. Yasmin, you should have known leavin' Miss Sandra alone with the kids was just not smart. She's unstable."

Having finished lecturing for the moment, she went into her bedroom and slammed the door.

I couldn't take it anymore. I just sank down in a chair and cried out, "Lord, I didn't mean to overstep, but I just felt like she was pushing me and making me feel bad because I didn't think of everything. Miss Sandra was slick. Yeah, she wanted to see her kids, but she didn't have to run off with them. If I had to do it all over again, knowing what I know now, I wouldn't have made the same decision. But how was I to know?"

Jada hugged me and went to check on Angel. I was so hurt. Then she came back and told me it was gonna be okay.

A little while later, Mom came out of her room. "Tell me everywhere you looked," she said. "I just called John and he was shouting all in the phone at me."

I started, "Well, I checked around the—"

"Are they back?" my brothers asked as they suddenly came busting in the door.

I just put my face in my hands because I couldn't tell them what they wanted to hear.

Jada was feeling my pain as she put her arms around me again. "You did what I would've done, Yasmin. You didn't know she was gonna do this."

"If she hurt those kids, I don't know how I'm gonna live with myself. It's all my fault," I cried out. "I'm so sorry!"

"I just don't know if being sorry is enough this time, Yasmin," Mom said.

That really hurt me; but this time I knew that I deserved it.

❦

"Okay, where are my kids? Have y'all found out anything?" Uncle John came running in the house, demanding answers. Aunt Lucinda was right behind him.

"Try to calm down, John. I called the police," Mom told him.

"I called the police too. Why ain't they here yet? I mean, what did Sandra say? What was she doin' with them?"

Mom sounded a little cool when she answered, "I wasn't here. You'll have to ask Yasmin."

Aunt Lucinda couldn't stop crying. "I know she wouldn't hurt those kids, but where does she live? Are they gonna be on the street tonight? They love being tucked in their beds with their teddy bears. We've got to find them. Honey, I told you we didn't need a date night. She needs to bring them back home now!"

My uncle came over and scolded me. "Yasmin, what were you thinkin'?"

Surprisingly, Mom came to my defense. "Ain't no need to jump on my child, John. We did all we can do for now. The girl tricked Yasmin into thinkin' the kids were safe while she went away for a second to check on the baby. Let's just pray right now that they're okay."

"We looked everywhere," Yancy said to my uncle. "We knocked on strangers' doors and asked had they seen the kids or heard anything. But nobody knew nothin'. If she said that she had a so-called friend she was stayin' with close by, she wasn't tellin' the truth."

"I promise you, guys, she didn't have a car. She didn't. Aunt Lucinda, you have to believe that I didn't mean to put them in harm's way."

"I know you didn't, sweetie," she said, making me feel a little better.

I knew if we didn't find them, I just wouldn't be able to go on. At this point, all I could do was pray. *Lord, everybody around here's frantic and it's hard for me to even swallow. This is so scary. Please be with the kids right now and allow Miss Sandra to bring them back. I know they are her kids but they're not supposed to be with her right now. We don't know where Miss Sandra is living, so please help us find them. Lord, I'm so sorry!*

Mom came over and placed her arm around me. Wow, prayers are truly good. I wasn't even praying aloud, but somehow she knew. She just squeezed me tight.

"We're gonna figure this out. Everything will be okay," Mom reassured me.

Having her on my side and giving me the grace I didn't deserve made my heart slow down and skip a couple of beats. I was really thankful and trusting God to help us.

Finally, the police arrived. When we went out to meet with them, they were questioning me and pressing me to tell them everything I knew. I was holding on, trying to be strong for Randi and Dante.

Then while the police were recording the information, a car slowly pulled up in front of us. The back door opened and the kids came running from the backseat. The driver tried to quickly drive away but the police flagged the car down. When they made her get out of the car, Miss Sandra was irate.

"What y'all call the cops on me for? I just took the kids for some ice cream. I can't spend time with my babies? Y'all took them away from me illegally anyway!"

"We got court papers to prove you otherwise, Sandra. We should press charges against you for taking them," Uncle John said sternly.

"I'm just saying. The court didn't have any reason to take them in the first place," she argued.

I wanted to say to Miss Sandra, *How could you do this to me? Why did you put me in such a horrible position?* But all I could do was stand behind Aunt Lucinda as she hugged the little girl and boy. It was obvious that the kids were relieved to see their foster mother. I knew from the way they were shaking that something had made them uncomfortable being with their mother. By the look on their faces it seemed like someone had scared them.

The policeman said, "Ma'am, you can't just take the kids without permission. We could charge you with a crime, if these people want to press charges."

"Charge me with a crime for spendin' time with my own children?" Pointing at my aunt and uncle, she accused them. "They were neglecting my kids . . . going out on the town . . . should've been watchin' them. I wish you would—"

The policeman said, "The foster parents left them with a babysitter."

"Yeah, Sandra . . . someone you know . . . and you manipulated her," Mom interjected. "Girl, you slick. You scoped out my place and knew I was gone so you could pull some mess like this."

"I wasn't intendin' to take them like that but Dante asked me for some ice cream. What is a mama supposed to do when her baby asks for ice cream? I had a few dollars in my pocket. After we had ice cream, me and my friend took them to a store to get them a little toy. Goodness gracious, what's so wrong with that. Sue me."

Frustrated with the whole situation, Uncle John asked her, "What do you want from us, Sandra? You want some money so that you can leave these kids alone? It's not doin' them any good with you poppin' into their life off and on like this. If you ever try somethin' like this again, I promise you, I'll have you put in jail."

"You're not gonna tell me when I can visit my kids! They're my kids and I can come and get them anytime I feel like it. I'm sick and tired of y'all tellin' me when I can and can't see them. I know what's best for them. Y'all are always threatenin' to lock me up whenever I wanna come around my children!" Sandra said, yelling into Uncle John's face.

At that moment, the kids started crying. They didn't need to be around this mess. It wasn't their fault that the adults in their life were dragging them through this ordeal. It hurt their feelings to see their mom all upset. After all, she was their mom.

"Ma'am, these people have custody of the children. You're going to have to take this matter up with the Department of Children and Families," the policeman said, pulling her away from Uncle John. "You have to calm down immediately. There is no need for you to be shouting and upsetting the children," the officer told her.

Miss Sandra didn't seem to understand, and she kept getting louder and acting crazier. So Aunt Lucinda took the kids into our house to get them away from the madness. The police proceeded to escort Miss Sandra to her car and told her if she didn't leave peacefully, then they were going to take her to jail immediately. She finally got into the car and left with her friend.

As they prepared to leave, one officer turned and said to my uncle, "Sir, you all need to work this out and do what's best for the children. I am certainly going to file a report about their mother's behavior. You might consider filing a restraining order against her. Clearly, the woman doesn't understand how much distress she has caused these innocent children tonight. By being exposed to this traumatic experience, their sense of peace and security was threatened. In my book, the disrupter never prevails."

# Chapter 4

# Calmer
## Feelings Rule

On Sunday morning, I was the first one up—dressed and ready to go to church. God had come through for me in a big way. The kids were okay. Even though a lot of what happened was completely bad judgment on my part, the outcome could have been terrible—but it wasn't. I had to thank God for protecting those kids.

When I peeked into Mom's room, she was sound asleep. I closed the door and went to check on my brothers. Although I was very angry with them for being overly friendly with my friends and not telling me, I did appreciate the fact that they had scoured the neighborhood trying to help find Randi and Dante.

I knew the one thing that would get everybody up was for me to fix breakfast. My thoughts went back to weekends when Jeff Jr. was alive. We had so much fun making pancakes, scrambled eggs, grits, and toast with jelly. As I started cooking, good memories about him flooded my mind. Suddenly all the tenseness from the night before started to slip away. The weight of the world I felt on my shoulders lifted. My deep disappointment in myself disappeared.

I just smiled. I wanted to believe my brother was standing right next to me saying, *"So last night was crazy, huh? You got a big heart, Yasmin. You always have. Just don't let anyone take advantage of you. That's what happened to me. I got pulled in so many different directions that I broke."*

"How do I not break?" I asked out loud as though I was talking back to him.

*"You got to open up the Bible. You got to let God lead you. So many people run to Him after the fact. They look for God when they're in trouble and need Him to help them find their way out. But seek Him daily and help everybody in this family do the same. I'm proud of you, little sis."*

The sound of the eggs frying and popping in the grease caught my attention; they were sticking to the pan. I glanced back to where I imagined my brother had been standing and the image was no longer there. Suddenly, I was back to reality. Yes, my brother was gone and I sure did miss him. But somehow I knew he was still with me, helping me to be strong.

"Breakfast is ready!" I called out.

I didn't have to call twice for York or Yancy. They were pulling each other back to get to the table first. Mom didn't get up, though, so I put her food on a plate, poured some orange juice, and took it to her in bed.

"Mom, I made breakfast. Can we go to church this morning?"

"Naw, I don't feel good. I appreciate you making breakfast, but it's a lot going on right now. Not today for me, okay?"

I wanted to say, *But church is where we can get a message to turn things around. You need to go to church if you're feeling down because that's where you can get lifted up.* But I could tell from her puffy eyes that she was dealing with something heavy. She and Dad hadn't spoken in a while, at least not from what I could tell. I didn't know if they were having problems; she hadn't mentioned anything to me. So I just stayed in my place and didn't ask.

"I understand," I said to her, wanting to be obedient and remembering I needed to please God with every action.

Just as I was leaving her room, she said, "Call Uncle John. I know he'll come and get you if you want to go to church."

A lump came up in my throat. I didn't want to call Uncle John right after everything that happened Friday night. Mom knew me well enough and could sense my hesitation. She rolled over and picked up the phone. I was standing there shaking in her doorway. What if he rejected coming to get me? Was he really over it? I couldn't hear what he and my mom were discussing. Then she hung up the phone and told me that he and his family were on their way. Thirty minutes later my uncle was blowing his horn for me.

Uncle John was a deacon in the church; he and his family were regulars. I was very quiet on the ride over, and when we got to the church he opened the car door for me. He motioned for Aunt Lucinda to go on inside with the kids.

Then he said to me, "Yasmin, I was a little rough on you the other night, and I'm sorry about that. I know you were scared and you did everything in your power to track the kids down. They love you as a babysitter and we're thankful for how much you care for them. I just need you to accept my apology for my behavior. Now that I've had a chance to think about everything, I don't want you to think that I blame you."

All I could do was hug him. No words needed to come from my mouth because my heart was full. He could tell that I was thankful from my embrace. After that needed moment of relief, we hurried on inside.

I really missed attending my Sunday school class on a regular basis. It had been so long since I'd been there that we had a new teacher. There was a woman standing by the door and not a man. But my eyes gleamed with joy when I saw it was my old guidance counselor from elementary school, Mrs. Newman, who was also the pastor's wife. As soon as she saw me, she was excited too.

"Hey, lady, I miss you. You doing all right?" she said cheerfully.

"Yeah, I'm okay," I said hesitantly. "How've you been, Mrs. Newman?"

"I've been good. It's time for class to start now. We'll have to catch up soon. I'm glad to see you."

"It's great to see you too," I said, trying to hide my true feelings.

"Well, good morning, class. I'm Mrs. Newman. Today we will be talking about the Golden Rule: 'Do unto others as you would have them do unto you.'"

I was glad we were going to discuss this particular subject because a part of the reason I was upset had to do with my brothers being with my best friends. They weren't giving me the respect I thought I deserved. I wanted them to be able to tell me that they liked each other instead of hiding behind my back. But, then again, maybe I had to put the shoe on the other foot. How would I feel if it was the other way around and I was Asia or Perlicia?

Mrs. Newman finished the lesson by reminding us that the Golden Rule was about operating on the side of right. When we choose to do what is right, it shows we have integrity and people will respect us for that. We should always want people to treat us with respect and so we should do the same to them. Most of all, if right prevails then life is good. So I made up my mind that I was ready to practice this rule and planned to settle for nothing less in return.

⊰❦⊱

When Sunday school ended, Mrs. Newman called me over to her. "You been okay, Yasmin?" she asked. "I haven't seen you around. I know you're in high school now but I've just been thinking about you."

"Yes, ma'am. I've been trying to remember all the things you taught us in the L.I.G.H.T. group, and I've been trying to—" I paused.

"Yasmin, I can tell from your eyes that something's not right. Talk to me. What's wrong?" she said.

"It's this whole thing about treating others as you want others to treat you. I don't know. I feel like so many people in my life don't care at all about what I think or feel. Even though I try to treat them with the right heart, they couldn't care less about how they treat me."

She tried to help me understand. "Well, you have to talk to people in a way that's not confrontational. You've got to let them know that you care about their views as well as your own. And it's okay to let out what you feel inside, because if it stays in, you never deal with it. Then you create an even bigger mess. Peace, true peace, can only come when you are honest with the people in your life and you are honest with yourself. Then again, it can't be a screaming match. There is no peace in that kind of communication; nothing gets accomplished. Neither person hears or understands what the other is trying to say."

I listened closely because I really wanted to get this. She continued. "Do you understand what I'm saying, Yasmin? Here's my number; stay in touch. Call me anytime. And if you ever need a ride to church, let me know that as well. I want to see you around here more."

"Yes, ma'am. Thanks for caring about me enough to talk to me."

"Thank you for being a remarkable young lady who can sustain tough times and still come out shining. I'm proud to know you," she said as she gave me a hug.

After church, my uncle asked me if I wanted to go out to dinner with him and his family. I still felt a little awkward being around them after what had happened so I just said "no, thank you" and asked him to take me home. I kinda regretted that decision because as soon as we stepped in the door we heard Mom fussing at my brothers.

"I don't know what we gonna eat! I'm tryin' to find something now."

"Why don't I go and pick up a box of chicken and bring it back?" Uncle John offered.

"Yeah, that's great!" Yancy said, smacking his lips at the mere mention of fried food.

"I don't need no handouts, John," Mom said in a harsh tone.

"It's okay, Yvette. I was just tryin' to help." He turned to my brothers and said, "Anyway, y'all know I could've taken you to church this morning too. Boys, just call me anytime. It's never a bother. I don't mind at all."

For some reason, Mom was acting really on the defensive. As though he had been talking to her, she responded, "Listen, John, I don't believe you got to go to church *every* Sunday. I wasn't feelin' well and I just didn't make it today. But thanks for takin' Yasmin," she said in a really upset voice. I just didn't understand where she was coming from these days.

"No problem. I figured with all that Yasmin's been through, she probably felt like she needed to be closer to the Lord," he responded.

Mom ignored him and turned her attention to me. "Did you get something out of the service?" From the sound of her voice, she was clearly upset with the whole situation.

Not wanting to make her even more angry, I calmly said, "Yes, ma'am. It was great."

Uncle John wasn't finished yet. "Well, I apologized for my tone with Yasmin the other night and, Yvette, I just wanted to go ahead and apologize to you too."

"You know, it's funny. People like you who go to church every Sunday should be the ones tryin' to help people be better. But as soon as some real pressure came, you were goin' off on my child. You're a deacon, aren't you? You're supposed to set the example. So what's the point of me going if I'm gonna act like you act?" Mom said angrily.

"All right, you're right. Call me out. But just because I'm a deacon don't mean I'm perfect. That's why I go to church—to get better. Obviously, you got a lot on your mind and I don't wanna intrude. I'd better go."

"Okay, well, you can leave now."

"Mom!" Yancy shouted.

Uncle John started toward the door. He waved good-bye as he was about to leave. Yancy looked so sad, and I felt bad for him too.

Before Uncle John could close the door, York took the chance and went over to Mom and tried to reason with her. "Ma, he said he was gonna get us some chicken. You scramblin' here, tryin' to figure out what we gon' eat. You got the phone off the hook because you don't want the creditors to call. What's wrong with lettin' him help us?"

Knowing that he was right, my brother's words made Mom change her mind. "All right, John, if you can bring the chicken back that will be good." Then she turned to us, "I don't want to hear no arguing out of y'all either. I just don't feel good right now so don't nobody go nowhere and don't nobody bother me." With that, she walked back to her room and repeated her routine of slamming the door shut.

"She's so mad. It seems like she knows we've been hangin' out with some girls or somethin'," Yancy said, looking over at me. He must have been dealing with some strong guilt feelings.

"Don't look at me. I didn't tell her anything."

York chimed in. "Yeah, I don't think Yasmin told her anything. Mom's just been actin' real weird lately. I tried to get in touch with Dad and his cell is disconnected, so I don't know what's going on."

Now was the time for me to bring up what was bothering me. "But since you brought up the girls," I said, "how could y'all do that and not tell me?"

York answered first. "We don't have to tell you everything, Yas."

"Yeah, that's obvious. But we talked about this. We agreed that you guys would never talk to any of my friends ever again. Remember what happened with Veida? And, speaking of her, what do you think she's gonna say about this? She still likes both of you guys."

"Veida ain't got no claim on me," York called out.

"Ditto that. It was you who set some boundaries between us and your friends," Yancy explained. "York and I didn't agree to anything. We thought you were just babbling."

"What! Babbling?" I sounded off pretty mad.

"That's why we didn't tell you 'cause we knew you would over-react just like you're doin' now," York said. "Besides, your girls are cool. They've been liking us for a long time. It's no surprise that we like them too; things have changed." York started smiling. He was suggesting that their bodies had developed more. Clearly, my brothers weren't still into climbing trees and making mud pies, like in the good old days. Now they've started acting like they're ready for grown-up relationships.

Then Yancy laughed and said, "Yeah, you know they're more mature now . . . much cuter . . . not so silly."

"Yeah, yeah, that's what I'm talkin' about," York smirked.

Then the two of them gave each other a high-five. I had to admit to myself that the bonding they were doing was cool. It was just that they were connecting about stuff I wasn't ready for them to bond on.

I was determined for them to hear me out and I was just getting started. "Well, you see, this is the problem. I need to let you know how I feel about it. They're my friends. If anything goes wrong with your relationships—and since we're all so young, something's probably gonna—then I won't have my friends anymore. They'll feel awkward comin' around here because of how things went with you two. I'm just saying, before you went there and encouraged them, you could have at least brought me in on it. At least, that's what I would've done for y'all. They are my girls, and I don't want to lose them. But if they choose you guys over me—I know it's gonna hurt."

Both my brothers were silent. I knew they were taking in what I said. I couldn't keep them from being friends with Perlicia and Asia, but I knew they had heard me. At the least they would take my feelings into consideration—and that meant a lot.

The next day in school Asia and Perlicia came up to me, yanked me by the arm, and hemmed me up in a corner.

"Okay, so what you been tellin' your brothers?" Perlicia demanded with her head rolling from side to side.

"Yeah, Yasmin, what's the deal? I mean, I finally get a boy who really likes me and you tryin' to block," Asia complained. "Yancy wouldn't even talk to me or walk me to class. He acted like he didn't even want to be seen next to me. Did you say somethin' to him, Yasmin?"

I smiled inwardly. I guess the smile showed up on the outside too. The thought of them being apart from my brothers made me happy.

"Oh, so you think this is funny?" Perlicia asked when she saw that I couldn't contain my grin.

"No, no, I don't think it's funny. I'm just sayin'. . . . I mean, I didn't tell them . . . whatever . . . I don't know."

"You do know. Stop trippin' over your words. Tell us what you said so we can send you to do damage control," Perlicia commanded me. "The truth is, we couldn't tell you because you and

Myrek are havin' issues about you movin' away and everything."

"Yeah, and we didn't want to make you feel even worse about it all," Asia added.

"Exactly. Now, be a good friend and share what you told your brothers," Perlicia interjected. She was holding her hands tightly around my wrists.

Just then Veida showed up. "What are you doin' with your hands on Yas like that?" she asked.

The smile left my face quicker than a remote can change the TV channels. I realized that my girl had no idea what shocking info she was about to be told.

"Oh, we just messin' around with Yasmin," Perlicia playfully admitted.

"I thought you two were gonna spend the night with me after the game. What happened? Did y'all go over to Asia's? Or did y'all go to Yasmin's house?"

"Nope, they weren't with me," I quickly responded. I wanted the record to show that I wasn't the mastermind behind them being involved with my brothers.

Asia and Perlicia were both silent. I waited to see if they were going to tell Veida the truth or make up some outrageous story.

When none of us said anything, Veida started to get suspicious. "What are the three of y'all hiding from me? I feel like y'all have left me completely out of the loop about somethin'," Veida said. It was obvious that she was getting a little salty.

I thought to myself, *You have no idea how much "out of the loop" you truly are.* I just looked at my other two friends—stared them down, actually. They needed to come clean; they needed to tell Veida the truth. Instead, they both looked away. But like clothes hanging on a rack, I was not lettin' them off the hook.

Finally, Perlicia spoke up first, "I'm just gonna say it."

"No no no! Don't do that!" Asia pleaded with her.

"Say what? Don't say what? I'm so confused. Talk to me, please," Veida pressed.

"Class is about to start, you guys. We gotta go," Asia cut in. She was really anxious to break up the conversation.

As for me, I didn't want to let it go. So I added, "I just feel like, if somebody is that nervous about givin' information, they must have a guilty conscience. That means they shouldn't be doin' whatever they're doin', and tryin' to hide it."

"Okay, you guys are really scaring me," Veida admitted. "Will somebody *please* talk to me?" she asked, sounding desperate.

"Nothin', it's no big deal," Perlicia answered.

"Oh, you think it's no big deal? Then tell her," I charged. I kept pressing, unable to stay out of it.

In fact, I was very much in it. If we were all going to remain friends, we had to care about each other and treat each other like we wanted to be treated. To keep Veida in the dark about something she was so connected to—was just wrong.

"Okay, here it goes," Perlicia finally said. "Just in plain language, Asia and I have boyfriends."

Veida said nothing.

"You wanted to know; I thought you'd be happy for us," Asia added.

"I knew y'all had boyfriends. It's no big deal," Veida stated. "You two were grinnin' too wide at the game. It's got to be some varsity basketball players, huh? If I could just get York or Yancy to like me, I would have a boyfriend too. I mean, I still like both of them. . . . It's crazy."

"They aren't gonna like you anyway. They like us." Perlicia just blurted it out. "I'm talkin' to York and Asia's talkin' to Yancy."

"What?" Veida responded. It was as if she heard everything they said but didn't want her mind to take it all in.

Her eyes were tearing up and so were Asia's. Perlicia stood her ground and grinned. I said nothing. These three were my girls and I didn't wanna step outside my boundaries. Now that the secret was out, I didn't need to get into their business. This wasn't my battle so I watched from the sidelines.

Veida was heartbroken. "You guys knew how I felt about them and now you're talkin' to them. I thought we had a sisterhood. I thought we had a strong bond. How could you do this to me?"

"I'm so sorry," Asia apologized as tears started falling from her eyes.

"Well, I'm not sorry," Perlicia said with her lips pouting. "They like us; we like them. That's just how it is."

"Yeah, go ahead and look out for yourself," Veida said to her. "Forget my feelings."

"Feelings? You can't bounce back and forth between both of them any time you want. One day it's Yancy; the next day it's York. You tore them apart as brothers. Now the two of them hang out together when they're hangin' out with us. We didn't want to tell you because we didn't want to hurt your feelings."

"Obviously, you don't care about my feelings that much because you hurt them anyway. Fine. Go ahead and have York and Yancy. Don't you ever call me again, thinking we're still friends. And don't expect me to have your back. I'm through with both of you!"

Before anyone said another word, Veida walked away.

"What?" I asked when they looked at me like it was all my fault.

"You pushed me to tell her," Perlicia said to me. "What people don't know sometimes can't hurt them. I mean, you've gotta admit I was right. All she ever did was pull your brothers apart. And what would stop it from happening if they got involved with her again? They were a mess and everybody knew it. The four of us aren't gonna be joined at the hip anymore, but we got your brothers' best interests at heart."

I tried to remember what Mrs. Newman told me, so I listened carefully to what Perlicia was saying. But I also had to share with her how I felt about this in my heart.

So I told her, "You know, we had a cool foursome going. We did have a sisterhood. I didn't think about it like that until Veida just said it. Since I don't have any sisters, I would've given my shirt for y'all. Boys might like you one day but they don't like you the next. Think about it. Are my brothers worth messin' up the great friendship we had? I know y'all are into them right now, but Veida's hurt about this whole thing. We should all care about that.

"Besides, I'm worried that when York and Yancy break up with you guys, you aren't gonna want to hang out with me. Just think about the bond we've felt for each other. I believe when you give it some thought you'll at least understand where Veida and I are coming from. This ain't right. You'll see that when calmer feelings rule."

# Chapter 5

# Jumper
## to Conclusions

anners were posted all over the school, and everybody was excited. Our "Sadie Hawkins Valentine's Day Dance" was going to be a blast. Of course I had asked Myrek to go with me. We'd been cool the last couple of weeks, but we hadn't had any real conversation. Yes, we were together, but Myrek was still sulking. I figured he was probably trying to face the fact that we would be breaking up when it was time for me to move away. I understood because I was having trouble with it myself.

His dad dropped us off at the dance, along with my brothers. It didn't take a rocket scientist to figure out that Perlicia and Asia would be waiting for York and Yancy to get there. But everyone was surprised when we walked in and saw Veida. I could tell that Perlicia and Asia didn't know how to handle it.

After all, Veida had told them that she didn't want to be friends anymore. I had tried to call her, but she hadn't returned my calls. Since I was hanging out with the girls and she was no longer cool with them, she was going to make me an enemy too. But what was I to do? It didn't seem like much of a crew without her.

"I'm gonna go over and talk to Veida. Okay?" I said to Myrek.

"Go ahead. Do whatever," he said rather harshly as he shrugged his shoulders.

Naturally, my feelings were hurt. I mean, I hadn't done anything to him. So what was wrong now? Lately, I'd been the sweetest girlfriend I could be. He had my full support at his basketball games. I had even done as he requested and was staying away from Billy. I was really into us. Why wasn't he into me?

After shooing him off like an annoying fly, I went over to Veida and said cheerfully, "Hey!"

I was trying to be a little over-the-top on purpose, wearing the widest smile I could make. Veida didn't return the gesture; she quickly turned away and walked in the opposite direction. So I jumped in front of her to keep her from getting away.

"Wait! Wait! Please don't tell me you're mad at me," I said to her. She looked at me as if to say, *Are you kidding?*

I persisted. "Can we talk, please? I mean, I didn't think I would see you here, but since you are—" I uttered. Instantly, I wished I could take it back because this time she walked away, rolling her eyes.

I wouldn't let her go. "No, Veida, don't take it the wrong way. I'm not saying that I'm not glad you're here or that you're not supposed to be here," I explained. Still, I wanted to kick myself, even in the lavender, sparkling, spaghetti-strapped gown that I was wearing. Although it had come from the secondhand shop, it was still a sacrifice for Mom. But I really loved it; it made me feel like a princess.

"I'll probably have to hang out with you anyway because Myrek's trippin'," I continued.

Still I got no response.

"All right, Veida, if you want to be like that and act salty all night, then go ahead. You can't even see that I care about you. Fine. Be that way."

Finally, she let me have it. "You know what? I would rather be by myself if I have to wonder whether the relationship is true and worry my head off about whether my best friend is stabbing me in the back or not. I can't believe you're hangin' out with Perlicia and Asia. You should be mad at them too for hookin' up with your brothers."

Veida wasn't finished yet. "But no, y'all are walkin' around thinkin' you're the hottest couples in school and I'm not a part of that. Okay? So just leave me alone. I wanted to come to the dance tonight but maybe it was a mistake. Anyway, since I'm here, I plan to have a good time. And I can't have a good time if I'm being with someone totally fake like you."

She walked away from me for the last time of the evening and I could barely breathe. I was extremely sad after hearing those very painful words.

I guess I looked kinda crazy standing in the middle of the room watching Veida walk away. The next thing I knew, Perlicia and Asia came up on both sides of me. I wasn't paying them any attention because I was still thinking about Veida. *Where had our friendship gone?* I wondered. I cared for her and she thought I had dogged her. That hurt!

Perlicia said in a mean tone, "Good riddance. She always thinks the spotlight is on her anyway. It's about time someone shows her that it's not."

Asia put her arms around me sympathetically and said, "I'm bummed. I understand her being mad at me but now she's mad at you too. She'll come around. But right now you can't worry about her. Your date is over there looking pitiful and you need to handle that."

"I don't know what's going on with him. He was being all stuffy in the car too," I said.

"Well, it can't be about how you look," Perlicia said. "You look so cute. I've never seen your hair put up like that. My girl is fly; for sure."

"Yeah, thanks. His sister, Jada, hooked me up."

"Well, we're gonna dance with your brothers," Perlicia declared. "Mope, if you want."

"Don't make Myrek feel bad that he came," Asia said to me before walking off with Perlicia. "Dance and have fun."

I followed them over to the boys. York and Perlicia started complaining about the slow jams and asked the DJ to play some fast songs. Yancy and Asia walked slowly, hand in hand, to the dance floor. I motioned for Myrek to come and dance, but he didn't move.

"You wanna talk?" I asked. He didn't respond. "Could you please tell me what's wrong with you? What did I do now?"

"I don't know. It's not really anything that you *did*. It's just that I can't figure out how we're supposed to get closer. You're acting as if I'm not supposed to be bothered that you're about to leave in a little while. I don't know. I just don't think this is working. Let's quit tryin' to act like everything is cool between us. You know why? Because knowin' you're about to leave makes none of this cool with me."

"What are you saying?" I asked as tears filled my eyes.

"I don't know what I'm saying!" he shouted back at me.

I just took one long look at him and then I couldn't look at him anymore. At that moment, I ran toward the exit and into the hall—away from everybody.

Dashing to the girls' restroom, I prayed, *Lord, this is hard. Myrek and I decided that we would remain friends and even try to stay close when I moved to Orlando. Then tonight, out of the blue, when I wanna feel like a princess, he makes me feel like an ugly stepsister. This hurts and I wanna be tougher. Please let me not stay down. In Jesus' name, I pray. Amen.*

As I approached the door, I ran into one of the twins. It had been a while since I'd had to deal with either of them and I was glad. One is supercool and the other is a jerk, and I didn't want to get them mixed up again. Nor did I wanna give Myrek anything to get upset about, not that I thought he cared. But now I was confronted by the guy in front of me. At first, I thought he might be the cutie with a mean streak and I wasn't about to get bummed out any more than I already was.

"Excuse me," I said to him, trying to go around him and handle my business.

"What are you runnin' away from?" he asked.

I ignored his question. "I said, excuse me. Please let me by," I replied, pushing past him.

"You look really pretty," he said, giving me a compliment.

Judging by his remark, I was sure he was Billy. "So you're Billy," I said out loud.

"Yeah. Hi, Yasmin. You look sad," Billy said, in a gentle way. "I stayed away for the past few weeks because I respect the fact that you have a boyfriend. But I gotta be honest, Yasmin Peace, I've been watchin' you and I just think that dude you hang with is more into himself than he's into you. I mean, here you are at a dance, looking all beautiful on the outside. You should be enjoying your-self, but I can tell everything isn't what it seems to be. I would have you smiling if you were my girl."

Now, how was I supposed to respond to that? I agreed with him. My boyfriend wasn't treating me right and it was too obvious!

"Well, thanks for the small talk," I responded, for lack of any-thing better to say.

"No problem. If you ever need me, call me," he said as he reached out to give me a hug.

I reached out to hug him back. But it sorta felt weird with him holding me so tight. I wanted to say, *You can let go now, Billy.* Then as the hallway suddenly filled up with people, I tugged away quickly. Too many oohs and ahhs filled the space. Perlicia and Asia were the first to run up to me.

"Didn't you come here with someone else?" Perlicia rudely asked me.

"Can I borrow your cell phone?" I asked Asia. I was intention-ally ignoring Perlicia's smart remark. I went over to a corner and called my mother to come and get me.

"I don't understand," she said. "Are you hurt? Is something wrong? I can't believe you want to come home from a party this early. Did something happen between you and Myrek? He didn't try anything with my baby, did he?" Mom spouted question after question.

"Mom, please. I'm just ready to go," I huffed.

"All right, well, I'll be there as quick as I can."

I handed Asia back her cell phone and walked toward the front entrance of the school.

"Hey, Yas, where are you going?" Yancy caught up with me and asked. "Asia said you want to go home. Ma might make us go home early because you're not feelin' good. You know she's not gonna ride up here twice."

I snapped, "Well, then ride back home with Myrek like you always do. Instead of you worrying about your sister's feelings, all you care about is you leaving a dance early. I'm sorry for cuttin' into your fun. It's not any fun for me and I wanna go home. Okay?"

"All right, then. What's up with you?" Yancy said, walking away as though I had hurt his feelings.

Myrek wasn't far behind. "You're leaving?" he asked.

I couldn't believe he was asking me that. "You're the one with the attitude. I hope you weren't expecting me to stay," I said in an unusually loud voice.

"What? Are you tryin' to embarrass me? If you don't wanna stay, fine. There are plenty of girls who'll dance with me."

"Like I care," I told him, not meaning the words that came from my mouth.

He turned around and walked away too. I wanted so badly to tell him *I'm sorry,* but I had to be strong. Yeah, he was my best friend, but I couldn't let him walk all over me. I didn't know what he meant when he said that he needed to reevaluate how close we were getting since I was moving. But I needed to keep my feelings in check. If he kicked me to the curb tomorrow, I would still be standing tall.

When I got into the car with my mother, I just looked out the window. It didn't even matter that I couldn't see anything. The night sky was pitch dark and ugly like a bad storm was heading our way. Before she could say anything, I turned to her and said, "Mom, please don't make the boys leave early. They'll just blame me for making them have to leave too."

"I'm just sayin'. They know I won't be coming back over here two or three times in one night. They'll just have to get a ride with Myrek."

We pulled into the driveway after riding home with only the sound of our rattling car being heard. Before we went inside, Mom questioned me more while she stroked my hair.

"I wanna know what's going on, Yas. I figure it had to be really bad for you to call me to pick you up early from the dance. Did you and Myrek break up? Is it that same Raven girl?"

"Mom, I really don't wanna talk about it. Besides, Raven has been a nonissue."

She just grabbed my hand and started to pray, "Lord, just help my baby. Only You know what's wrong and only You can fix it."

That made me smile because it put everything in perspective. I was ready to go on. We had asked the Lord for help. And Mom was right—only He could fix it.

⋙◦⋙

On Saturday morning I woke up to Yancy beating on my door. "It's the phone for you, Yasmin. Get the phone!"

I rushed to the living room and picked it up. Yancy hadn't told me who it was, so I just said, "Hello?"

"Girl, I know y'all don't have a computer, but you need to hurry over to my house. You're all over this site!" Asia said excitedly, without even saying hello back.

"Yeah, you and Billy!" I heard Perlicia yell out. "And Myrek is *mad* about it!"

"I don't know what y'all are talkin' about," I told them.

"You just need to hurry over to my house," Asia repeated with urgency.

I had to think fast. Mom had already left the house. But thankfully her cell phone was working again. I quickly called her to see if I could go over to Asia's house. Of course she grilled me with about fifty questions, checking to see if Asia's mom was home. She told me to be home before dark since I was walking over. She wanted to make sure no boys were over there, and all kinds of stuff. When she heard all the right answers, it eased her mind. So she gave me the green light to go.

Perlicia had spent the night with Asia. For as long as I could remember, the two of them had always been really close. But I was really glad when we built a friendship with the three of us and Veida. Now it was just the two of them again in a tight relationship.

I couldn't get over there fast enough. When I arrived, they were waiting with the door wide open.

Asia quickly pulled me inside. As we walked to her room, she couldn't wait to say, "Come and look at this!"

When I looked at the computer screen, I couldn't believe what was before my eyes. It was a picture of me in Billy's arms! People from our school were online blogging about it. I read as quickly as I could: *She came with one guy and was in the arms of another. Does Myrek know where his girlfriend is?*

There had to be about thirty postings about me. What nerve!

I was hot with anger! Everybody was blowing this way out of proportion. Yeah, the hug went on a little too long. But who took a picture? Who posted it? And what was the big deal anyway?

"Girl, this doesn't look good," Perlicia said. "You didn't even stay the whole night. Myrek was so embarrassed; folks were talkin' up a storm!"

"I don't know why he was embarrassed. He told me that he would be dancing with tons of girls."

"He didn't really mean that," Asia added. "He only said that so you would stay and make sure he didn't. But it didn't work out that way. He was walkin' around looking so pitiful all night."

But I wasn't feeling pitiful at home because Mom had prayed for me, and the Lord allowed me to have a peaceful sleep. However, I did feel bad about the way we left things. I had gotten loud with him, and he had said some mean stuff to me. But did we mean any of it? I didn't. What happened to that great relationship we used to have before the boyfriend-girlfriend feelings got all mixed in with it?

"I think you better call him up," Asia suggested.

"No, she don't need to call him. She needs to go around there and get this mess straightened out," Perlicia spoke forcefully. "You need to see him because right now he's looking like a real jerk on this thing!"

Then a message popped up from Myrek: *I don't care what Yasmin Peace does.*

When it appeared, I couldn't believe he just wrote that. My heart was torn into a million pieces. Was he agreeing with all these people about all this Billy drama? I didn't even know Billy that well. And I had done all I could to stay away from him so there wouldn't be any misunderstanding. But the one time I did talk to the guy and he gave me a hug and a compliment—something my boyfriend, who by the way had made me feel like junk, wouldn't do—all of a sudden I have to read that Myrek doesn't care what I do.

"Yeah. I'm goin' around there," I said. "I'm tired of tryin' to figure it all out. Myrek told me that he didn't know where we stand. And now that someone shows me some attention and he heard about it on a website, he wanna diss me."

"I don't think you should give him a piece of your mind," Asia advised. "That may not be the angle to play."

But Perlicia egged, "No, you need to tell him that you don't appreciate him gettin' on the Internet and tellin' people that he don't care what you do."

It was time for me to go. I found out everything I needed to know and the two of them really needed to stay out of it. So in my mind, I just blocked them out of my head. I was hoping that Myrek was heading to the basketball court because I couldn't go over to his place. My mother had already told me to go over to Asia's and then go home. But the basketball court was on the way, so I wasn't really disobeying her. Maybe I was pushing it a little, but Mom also taught me not to be a wimp. Myrek needed to hear from me on this.

When I got to the court, he was already working on his free throws. I went over and confronted him, "You were online a few minutes ago, weren't you?"

"You've been all over the Internet today. So what?" Myrek challenged me as he threw another basket.

Ignoring that, I asked him, "What was that comment about you not caring what I do?"

"I meant what I said. You can be on there with Billy, his brother, and anybody else in the world. I don't care. You left me alone at the dance."

"I left you there because you were treating me like someone other than your girlfriend. You've been actin' like I don't care that I'm about to move, but you're wrong. Since you basically want us to break up just because I'm moving away, I'll go along with that. There, you happy? Is this what we're agreeing to?"

"I don't agree to nothin', but you were in somebody else's arms," he said, running after the ball.

"He just said some nice things to me. That's all."

"But think about how you would feel if the situation were reversed."

He had a point. I didn't like thinking about him being with Raven last semester. But I wasn't gonna give in to his point either.

"Well, think of how you would feel if I were mean to you and made you feel bad."

Myrek blurted out, "I didn't wanna break up. It's just I don't know how to deal with it. Losing you is hard."

"And I didn't wanna leave the dance last night," I admitted. "I just didn't wanna be around you when you were acting so different and cold toward me. That wasn't a good thing at all. I just thought you didn't wanna be around me anymore. Period."

He put the ball down under his foot and rocked it back and forth for a minute. Then Myrek pulled me to him and said, "No matter what, Yasmin, we should always treat each other with respect. We gotta give each other the benefit of the doubt, and both of us have to quit being a jumper to conclusions."

# Chapter 6

## Helper Needs Help

So, are we good?" I asked Myrek. As I waited for his response, I thought, *This could turn out to be a pretty good ending.* I could already feel so much stress disappearing.

He kicked the ball away, leaned over, and gave me a hug. "Yeah," he whispered. "We're real good."

But I wasn't quite satisfied yet. "And, it's official. We agreed *not* to break up?" I asked again, just to be sure.

"For right now, anyway. It just drives me crazy to see you with someone else."

"Ditto," I told him.

"What else is there for us to do?" At least Myrek was willing to work things out and I was relieved about that.

"What about when I move?" I looked away and asked.

"Can we just stay focused on right here, right now, please? I mean, no one knows what's going to happen tomorrow," he reasoned.

"Well, if we know we're agreeing to break up at some point,

then you can be prepared and I can be prepared, right?" I asked.

Then Myrek really opened up his heart to me. "I don't know, Yas. All of that sounds crazy. Let's just enjoy being happy now. My dad always says that's what's wrong with people: everybody wants what they don't have and are always lookin' for the next thing. They never really enjoy the moment and be thankful for what is right there before them.

"I gotta be honest with you, Yasmin. I'm learnin' this whole God thing because I've been watching you. I had to live all my life without a mom, and who else could I blame for that but God? I always thought, if He loved me, then there was no way He could let my mom die. And even though it's been hard without her, and I know my life would be better if she was here, I was blessed to have a father who stuck by me. Most of the kids at school don't have one. It's like God looked out for me even when I was so mad at Him. If I'm gonna learn to accept that He loves me, I gotta learn to trust Him with everything. That includes you."

I just smiled so wide. I couldn't believe Myrek was talking about the Lord like that. It was just so moving. Prayer really does work.

"Now, I need you to tell this Billy dude to keep his hands off my girlfriend. Or do I need to?" Myrek said sternly.

"See, you just got finished talkin' about God. How you gonna talk about handling business with violence?" I quickly reminded him.

"I ain't tryin' to fight him or nothin' like that. I'm just sayin' I do want you to get it straight. I love God and I feel like I'm growing in my relationship with Him, but I ain't no punk. I know God wouldn't want me to be one either."

"Now, don't try to put God in this business between you and Billy. You're just being jealous for no reason. I already squashed it and, besides, it wasn't what you think you saw. He just hugged me. That's it."

"And I want him to know that I don't want him touchin' my girl. What, you got a problem tellin' him that or somethin'?" Then Myrek ran after the ball again and picked it up. It was so strange. Whenever he wanted to run away from drama, he'd find a basketball and start shooting as if dribbling a ball could stop the tension.

"You gotta be able to trust me, Myrek."

"It's not you that I don't trust, Yas," he said while shooting a three-point shot. "What's the big deal? Why are you stressin' about talkin' to him? You like this guy or something?"

"No, I don't. And you know I don't. I just don't feel comfortable with you telling me who I can or cannot see. It's like you're tryin' to be my dad or somethin' and that's not cool."

"You didn't have any problem tellin' me I couldn't talk to Raven."

"That's because she wanted to be your girlfriend!"

"And I'm tellin' you that the Billy dude was hangin' on to you because he wanna take my place. And if you can honestly look at me and tell me that he didn't say anything that would prove what I'm sayin', then I'll back off. But I don't think you can do that."

At that point, I gave up. I just shook my head and started walking home. I was upset. Myrek should be able to trust me. But with every step I took, I replayed the night of the Sadie Hawkins dance, and Billy was being overly friendly. Now that I was thinking about it, he did tell me that he could be a better boyfriend. I had to let him know that Myrek and I were cool. I didn't want him to think that he and I could be anything more than friends. But Myrek didn't even want Billy and me to be friends. Was that going to be cool with me?

I just looked to the sky and prayed, *Lord, thanks for helping Myrek and me see things through. It's so hard being a teenager. I wanna please You and I want You to help me be happy. I just haven't figured out the key to what that is. Please help me figure out the way. Don't leave me stranded. Please, Lord.*

"No! Don't answer that phone!" Mom screamed out. The phone had been ringing off the hook. I was wondering why no one had picked it up, and I was just about to answer it when Mom stopped me.

"York, Yancy, get in here!" she called out.

"What's up, Ma?" York asked.

"I'm tired of y'all not pullin' your weight around here."

"What are you talkin' about, Mom?" Yancy said.

"I just got your report cards. Y'all always want this and that and you can't even do your part, but then you want me to go out of my way to get what you want. Y'all have to realize that it's tough times and you're gonna have to do better."

"Mom, I got straight As," Yancy reminded her.

"You got three 91s."

Yancy rightfully defended himself. "But you never cared before what the number grade was, as long as my final grade was an A."

Mom just ignored Yancy's answer and stared at York. "And your report card, I just don't know what to say."

Now it was York's time of defense. "I got a 59 in math last time and this period I got a 76. That's a C. You told me that you expect a passing grade."

"Well, a C is not good enough," she informed him. Then it was my turn. "Yasmin, you got all As and Bs but you know you can get straight As."

"Yes, ma'am," I said, not understanding where her frustration was coming from but rolling with it anyway.

Then she turned to the next thing. "Y'all can't even keep your rooms clean." She opened my room door and it was spotless.

"What's wrong with it, Mom?" I asked cautiously.

Pointing to my dresser, she said, "If I open up these drawers I know the clothes in there aren't as neat as they could be. And this closet," she continued, "look at those dirty clothes in there!"

I responded, "But, Mom, you haven't given me any money to do the laundry."

"Well, wash them in the sink and hang them up to dry. I don't have any change just lying around. You know you can't keep dirty clothes around here forever!"

It seemed like nothing we said would please her. The phone rang again and she ordered us not to touch it. I couldn't help but notice how much she was trembling. She'd avoided bill collectors in the past, but she seemed overly stressed about it right now.

Finally, Yancy asked, "Mom, why don't you want us to answer the phone? We can tell 'em you ain't got it."

"Please, you know they want their money; they'll just keep callin'," York cut in with a smart tone.

"Yes, and things ain't good for me right now. Those folks . . . I owe them and I'm gonna pay them. Times are just hard; that's all," Mom said. She was near tears as she slumped down in a chair.

"Ma, what's going on?" York asked. I could hear the concern in his voice.

I echoed, "Yeah, Mom, please tell us."

"Yeah, tell us what we can do better. Obviously, you're upset about somethin'. Your boss didn't give you the raise you wanted, huh?" Yancy questioned her.

Before she could answer, Yancy offered, "I can tutor after school and get paid for it."

"Yeah, and I can start back modeling," I chimed in.

"Where's Dad? He's not helpin' you through none of this?" York said bluntly.

She huffed, "Your dad doesn't need to know anything about what's going on right now. Okay?"

Suddenly, the phone rang again. She grabbed it and screamed into the receiver, "What! Yes, this is she. No, I don't have the money to pay it right now and I don't have anything to put on it. I lost my job. Now, who do I need to speak with so you'll stop callin' me? I'll pay you as soon as I can, but right now you ain't makin' my life easy!" Then she slammed down the phone.

I don't know what my brothers felt like at that moment. But I felt as if I was on a free-falling ride that had just shot downward with the speed of light.

York looked so upset. I knew he wasn't mad at our mother, but he was angry. "See, that's why I wanted to keep hustlin', Ma. It could help keep everything together."

Mom was trying to calm down and pull herself together. "I don't wanna hear any of that right now. Hustling is not the right way to solve our money problems. We'll find a way somehow. The Lord will help us through. I need to tell y'all that I got laid off because I was the last one hired, so I was the first they let go. I lost my job, but I didn't lose my hope. I've been lookin' everywhere, but no one's hiring right now."

"Then I'm gonna have to start hustlin'. I don't care what you say, Ma. I gotta hustle to help."

"And then what, York? End up dead like your old friend?"

"At least until I die we'll be eatin'. What's your plan?" he snapped back.

She raised her hand and slapped him. "My plan is I'm still your mama and I'm gonna find a way. That's my plan. I know you're in high school now, but you still ain't grown. All y'alls life y'all watched me struggle and I've never let you go hungry. This ain't nothin' new."

"Mom, why don't you call Dad? He doesn't know how bad it is. Even if he's in-between jobs, I'm sure he would do somethin' to try and help," Yancy pleaded with her.

"I—I—I just don't want him to think I can't do it alone."

Yancy kept at her. "But right now we need his help. You won't even know if he could or couldn't help, Mom, unless you ask him."

"I told you I got this, Yancy. See, that's why I didn't wanna tell y'all." Her pride was clearly getting the best of her.

Things were starting to add up. The news she just gave us made sense and prompted Yancy to say, "So that's why you've been around the house at weird times when you were supposed to be at work. Come on, Mom. How long have you not had a job?" he asked. York wouldn't look up; he had already suspected something was wrong.

She tried to take a positive attitude about it. "This is the third month; so bills are piling up on me. But our breakthrough is comin' soon. I just need y'all to hold it together. I'm sorry I've been fussin'

and kinda crazy, but it's gonna be okay. I believe it's gonna be okay."
Mom started crying as she hugged me. "It's gonna be okay, right?"
This was a strange moment; she was saying it and asking the question at the same time.

I looked at my brothers and we were all wondering the same thing. How in the world was it going to be okay? Here she was the adult, but she was crying like a baby. The three of us were going to have to figure out a way.

The next few days were really depressing; the phone was constantly ringing. But it wasn't our friends calling; neither was it someone calling about a job. It was just more bill collectors. It was making Mom really stressed. She sat us down and told us she had a lot of credit card debt.

Mom spelled everything out. She told us she had a gas card to get around, a department store card to buy us clothes, and a bank card for any other stuff that might come up. All of the cards were maxed out to their credit limit. Not only was she late on the car payment and the rent, she was behind on the credit card bills. With no job, we had no answers as to how everything would be fixed.

"Mom, they're taking the car!" York called out as he looked out the window.

She opened the front door and just screamed. It wasn't like she was screaming at the man to put the car down; she just yelled out the most horrific sound. I couldn't imagine it being worse if she was in physical pain.

Yancy rushed outside and tried to talk to the repo man. "Hey, please, don't take my mom's car. She needs it to get around. She's a hardworking lady. She hasn't paid 'cause she don't have a job right now, but she's gonna get a job. Please, you gotta understand, mister."

He was a big, scruffy-looking man who said, "Son, I understand your situation and it's unfortunate that your mother's car has to be repossessed. But if I don't do my job, then just imagine what would happen to me. I won't be able to feed my family."

"Yancy, you get back in here!" Mom called out. She was just getting off her knees. I was so busy listening to Yancy and the man talking, I didn't even realize that she was on the floor praying. Whatever she said to the Lord, I hoped He'd answer quickly because we needed His help right away.

Yancy obeyed Mom and started back inside. "Yancy, it's no need beggin' that man," Mom said to him. "There's nothin' he can do about it. I didn't pay my bill and I gotta suffer the consequences."

York seemed to have made up his mind. He pulled me aside and whispered, "I'm gonna have to hustle. She can't make it without a car. And when she does get a job, how is she gonna get anywhere? That's it. I gotta help out."

"No, you can't do that," I warned. "It's the last thing Mom would want."

"Ma ain't gotta know. You can keep your big mouth shut, right?"

"I think we need to open both our mouths and call Dad," I suggested.

"Yeah, what's up with that? What, did she ask him for money and he told her he didn't have it or somethin'?" York questioned.

"I doubt it's like that. She's just too prideful to ask him for help, I guess. We're all just like her in our own way."

York put on his shoes and headed to the door. Mom was coming out of her room just in time to ask him, "Boy, where are you going?"

"I'm just goin' to handle some things real quick, Mom. I'll be back."

"You better get in your room and handle pullin' those grades up. You think I'm gonna let you go out there and do somethin' illegal to bring some cash in here?"

"Well, Mom, let's face the facts. We don't have any cash now. Why should you care how we get it? You keep doing what you're doing and we'll be out in the streets. What, you gon' hit me again?" York challenged her.

The two of them stood toe-to-toe. Thankfully, to break the tension, there was a knock on the door. Mom looked at York and said, "I'll deal with you in a minute." When she turned around and opened the door, it was the landlord.

"I've left you several messages, Ms. Peace, and you didn't call me back. I also left notes on this door and you haven't responded to them. I'm sorry, but I have no other choice but to serve you eviction papers. You were given a thirty-day notice, but now you have one week before you have to vacate the premises," he stated very sternly.

She stepped outside the apartment and shut the door, but we could still hear her. "Look, I'm tryin' to get the money to pay you, but you can't kick me and my family out. I'm a good tenant here. You have to give me a chance to find the money."

"It doesn't work that way. If I allow you to stay any longer, then everybody around here will be paying when they want to. If I don't collect the rent, I'll be out of a job. This is strictly business," he responded.

"Where would me and my family go? I have a son in there right now thinking he has to help me. His only way is goin' out in the streets and gettin' into trouble."

"I don't want your son doing anything illegal, but let's be honest. A lot of people out here don't pay their bills with honest money. I know your son saved those kids' lives last year and you got a couple of free months' rent. Besides, you're paying for a two-bedroom when you're living in a three-bedroom. All of the charity's run out, Ms. Peace. Now, you've got seven days or your stuff will be out on the streets," he warned.

"Why do you hate me so much?" she asked.

"I don't hate you. Actually, I really feel sorry for you. I know you've had some big problems. But, as I said, this is business. You only have one week to pay the past-due amount and the current month's rent."

"Fine!" she yelled at him.

She came back into the house and slammed the door. Mom was trying to be strong. She said, "Don't worry. Everything will be okay, y'all. And, York, you better not make this worse and go hang out with them thugs. I'm sorry I hit you the other day, Son. I love you. I've never let y'all down before and I won't start now."

With that attempt to reassure us, she went in her room and closed the door. We heard her yell, "Lord, why is this so hard! I know You're gonna help me figure this out. I know You'll work this out for me and my kids."

Feeling frustrated and hopeless, both of my brothers went into their room. I just looked up and prayed, *Lord, we do need Your help. Mom's trying everything she can to make things work. She wants to find a job, but she needs a car. I know she's worried because our Mom wants to do her part. Lord, You are our Protector and Provider, but right now our helper needs help.*

## Chapter 7

# Stranger Things Happen

*T*he next few days had swiftly passed by. And tonight, for two main reasons, it was hard for me to sleep. First of all, we were experiencing the worst storm Jacksonville had seen this year. There was even a tornado warning in effect. Then too I could hear Mom constantly crying through the night. It looked like we had come to the end of our rope. The very next day we were to be out of the apartment.

This just didn't seem real, but Mom hadn't found a job yet and she hadn't come up with any rent money either. To make matters worse, the landlord wasn't letting up on the fact that we needed to be out. All I could do was pray and have faith that God would step in and do something quick; but honestly, day was breaking soon. Time was running out, and it was getting harder and harder to believe that we'd find a way out of this.

It must've been hailing outside because I woke up to the sound of constant tapping on my windowpane. When it wouldn't stop, I put the pillow over my head. But the noise just got louder and louder. I finally gave up and turned on my light. Just then I thought I heard a voice coming from outside.

"It's me, Yasmin! It's your dad!" The voice seemed to be calling out as the wind and rain cut through the sound.

I rubbed my eyes to make sure I wasn't dreaming. Then a knock on the front door startled me and I jumped to my feet. Who could it be this time of night? Was it Dad? Did I really hear his voice calling me? Had he come to help us?

"Mom! York! Yancy! Someone's knocking on the door! I think it's Dad!" I shouted.

By now I was pretty sure it was Dad, but just in case it wasn't, I hesitated to run straight to the door. I'd had my share of opening the door for the wrong person. A few months back a crazy neighbor had pushed his way inside. That experience made me extra cautious, so I waited for Mom.

She rushed into the room, wrapping her robe around her.

"What's all the noise about?"

"I think I heard Dad's voice and someone knocked on the door!" I told her.

Before Mom could get to the door, Yancy had heard me and he was rushing to open it. My father was standing there soaking wet.

My brothers and I were clearly excited to see him. But all Mom said as he stepped in was, "Who told you we were in trouble? You weren't supposed to come until you got that job you've been waitin' for. Did you get it? You didn't call me and say you got the job! Which one of you called your dad? I told y'all I didn't want him to know."

She went on for the next few minutes, accusing each of us one by one. As bad as I'd wanted to talk to my father, our phone was cut off a few days ago. We couldn't have called even if we wanted to.

It was so hard being poor. Just the bare necessities felt like perks that we had to live without.

Finally, my father saved us when he spoke to Mom. "I love you, 'Vette. I love these kids and I wanna help," he said as he handed her a roll of twenties. "Here's enough rent money for the past-due amount and this month too. I know you'll still need more, but we'll figure something out together and talk with the landlord. I can't believe you didn't call me, honey," Dad told Mom as he moved closer to her.

Mom couldn't hide the sigh of relief she was feeling as she accepted the money, but still she jerked away from him. "Wait a minute, Jeff. If none of the kids called you, how did you find out? Was it your big-mouth brother? Which one of y'all told your uncle what's been goin' on in this house?"

"Calm down, Yvette. Stop blaming the kids. This is about us."

"But I didn't wanna bother you with any of this, Jeff. You're trying to save money for the down payment on our own home. You already talked about how hard it is for you to save up anything because something always comes up. You also need to get your truck driver's license, and that costs money. Here, take this money back. You need to save it for our future."

Dad just looked at her and said, "Baby, if we can't get through the present, what kinda future are we gonna have? You think I'm gonna let my family be out on the streets? If I can't get my truck license now, it'll come at the right time. I did make a comment about it being hard to save money, but it's a joy for me to give it up for you guys.

"Right now I'm working a temporary job, but at least I'm working. It's been helping me to save money for my family and our future, and that's what's important. When I was locked up, I can't tell you how much I wished I could pay bills for you. And now that I can, it's yours. Why didn't you tell me that you lost your job, Yvette? You had me thinkin' that everything was okay."

"I just didn't want to put too much on you, Jeff. I was trustin' that God would make a way."

My father replied, "Well, I'm the way that He wants to use right now. Shouldn't we go through this together?"

By now Mom had clearly softened her tone and her demeanor. "You've just changed so much, Jeff. But I still wasn't sure how you would react. And I didn't wanna push you away."

"Baby, when you've been incarcerated and kept away from your family and the rest of the world, it makes you wanna deal with everyday problems. Whatever happens with you and these three affects me right here," he said as he pointed to his heart. "Together we stand, and we ain't gonna fall. But we're divided when you tell the kids not to tell me what y'all are dealin' with.

"When you keep things away from me, tryin' to handle it on your own, then it makes me feel like I can't provide for my family. I know I'm just gettin' on my feet, and I'm pretty much working eighteen-hour days. But just like I raised this money, I can raise some more. And know this, I can work twenty-four hours a day just to be sure I can keep a roof over you and these kids' heads. You're my family and you mean everything to me."

Then Mom buried her head in Dad's chest. She squeezed him real tight and started crying again—but this time it was a sound of joy. York was trying to act tough. He wasn't even smiling, but I saw his eyes begin to water.

Yancy patted Dad's back, thanking him for coming to our rescue. "I didn't know if you could help us, Dad. I didn't know what kind of financial situation you were in, but I knew if you could you would. Thanks, Dad."

Dad opened his eyes and pulled Yancy into a hug. "I remember two years ago on Thanksgiving Day when you came to see me in jail, Son. You didn't wanna have anything to do with your old dad. I promised myself then that, with everything in me, I would work hard to make you trust me again. We are a family and I'm here for you guys. After I talked to my brother, I got my money straight and drove here in a severe thunderstorm. I know it was dangerous, but if I had to do it all over again I would. Just to be with you guys. I love y'all," he said as he kissed Mom on the cheek.

She just smiled when he said he loved us. The strain had lifted; Dad had saved the day, and we were gonna be all right. Just an hour later, I fell into a sound sleep.

The next morning Mom was so happy, she was even making breakfast. There were cans of corned beef hash that had been in the pantry for who knows how long. She was whipping it up, along with some pancakes. Dad had gone to the grocery store to buy some eggs. They were the cutest things together in the kitchen, just laughing and playing.

"Come on in, you guys," she said to the three of us as we peered around the corner. We immediately took her up on the invitation.

"Dad, you gotta come around more often. She don't ever throw down like this!" York remarked. "Ma, you know I'm keepin' it real!"

"Oh, boy, hush," she said as she swatted her hand playfully at York.

"For real, Dad, we missed you. Can you stay with us a couple of days?" York asked.

"No, Son. I gotta get back to work."

"Man," Yancy said with disappointment. "I thought you could come out on the court with us and get some hoops in."

"See, I know y'all gon' want some new kicks in a minute. Dad gotta keep workin'."

"Right, right," York added. "Yep, that's what I'm talkin' about."

Mom was standing and watching us like she was holding a big secret. Her smile stretched from ear to ear as if she wanted to tell us some good news.

Yancy noticed it too. "What, Mom? What's goin' on?" he asked.

"Jeffery, you tell them. This is your idea so you tell 'em."

"Tell us," York pressed.

Mom couldn't hold it in any longer. She spoke first. "Well, okay. Your dad and I've been talkin'. We don't want him to have to keep on payin' for two households. Plus, the market isn't as bad in Orlando, so I have a better chance of finding a job there. Then too I could be closer to my mom. You guys have been doing so good; your grades will make it easy to transfer in the middle of the semester and—"

As she kept talking, I started to realize that Mom was saying we were going to move right away. I wasn't even eating yet, but I felt completely choked up.

"No, Mom!" I screamed out. "We can't move right now. It's bad enough that you're moving me away from my friends in a few months, but right now I'm in track season. We can't leave now!"

She said calmly, "I'm pretty sure whatever school you'll be attending down there has a track team." I was the one who was extremely excited.

"Yeah, but Coach Hicks really needs me on the team! And he's been in the Olympics before. The schools down there probably don't have a coach who can set me on a good path with track. He sees my potential and this is important to me. Mom, no! Please, no!"

Mom was stuck. She gave my father a look as if to say, *Can you help me, please?* But the look he gave her said, *You're on your own.*

"I don't think I'm ready to go either," Yancy spoke up. "I have all these honor classes and I know my teachers really well. I'll probably have to test into the honors program down there. I'm with Yasmin. I'm just sayin', y'all probably gonna do what you wanna do anyway, but I wanna say how I feel—"

"Boy, hush," Mom said, cutting him off. "You know you can get good grades at any school you attend. York, you might as well speak your mind. Yancy said it right, we're gonna do what we feel is best, but you can still give your opinion."

"I'm really not ready to move but . . ." He shrugged his shoulders as if to say *whatever.*

"Boy, you can be a little bit more respectful than that," Dad scolded him.

York quickly tried to explain himself. "I'm just sayin', Dad. It's the middle of the school year. We're about to have state testing soon. To move to another place right now . . . I don't like it. But if we gotta move, then we gotta do what we gotta do."

"Thank you, York," Mom said as though she really appreciated his words. I could've taken the plate she was fixing and thrown it upside my tough brother's head.

Then she turned to me and said, "Yasmin, it's not like I want to pull you away from track, your friends, or school right now. It's just there are so many other opportunities for us in Orlando. Plus, I miss my mom and I wanna help my sister take care of her."

I was still unwilling to let it go. So I said, "But, Mom, your sister isn't taking care of her. Big Mama is in a home."

"Well, my sister has to visit her all the time and I could spend more time with Mama if I was there. The three of you have each other. And don't forget, your cousins are there too."

"Yeah, cousins who cause a lot of trouble. Remember, Mom?" I said with some attitude. I was thinking back to last summer when I spent time in Orlando. My cousin Alyssa had gotten me into tons of trouble.

"Well, I'm sure if we let y'all decide, then we wouldn't be movin' anytime soon. But is that really what's right for this family? If we only have to pay for one household, your father and I could save more money. Besides, your dad doesn't want to spend time away from you guys any longer than necessary. Tell them, Jeff." Dad just nodded his head in agreement.

Still, I tried once again to be convincing. "If our phone was back on, we could call Dad more often. I know we need more money comin' in and you don't want York to mess with the guys in the neighborhood, so I'll call my old agent and get some modeling work. At least that's legit. It'll be bad enough when we have to move in June. Don't move me now, please!"

"You're movin', Yasmin Peace, so you might as well let the idea settle in your head. You need to cut it out. I see you actin' like it's gonna make you sick to your stomach. Your dad's goin' back today and we're goin' down there next week. You'll have a week to say good-bye to your friends. Kids have to move all the time. Get a better attitude and get over it. We're movin'. Period!" Mom said as though the case was closed.

Three days later, I was talking to Myrek while I packed my room. "Well, at least your phone's back on," he said to me.

I was trying to be the big girl and not cry anymore. Come to think of it, there was one bit of sunshine that getting ready to move positively did for me. Veida wasn't mad at me anymore. Don't get me wrong, I was getting my friend back but I wasn't gonna be able to enjoy it. After I moved to Orlando, the last thing I'd be trying to do is befriend anyone. Anyway, I'm sure they already have set cliques.

"Why are you so quiet?" Myrek asked when he noticed I wasn't saying anything.

"Oh, I was just thinking. Yeah, my phone is back on but we're about to leave. The only reason Mom turned it back on was so she could handle last minute business and communicate with my dad so they can straighten things out."

"Straighten things out with your dad? I don't know what you mean."

"You know, they're making arrangements for us to come down there like finding where we're gonna stay and enrolling us in school. Actually, he's supposed to be on his way here now. Mom's already asked me four times if my things are boxed up, but I can't seem to get it done."

"Are y'all leaving out today?"

"We might stay here through the weekend, but I don't know for sure. We gotta get settled so we can start school on Monday."

"I'm comin' over there. I wanna say bye."

"*Bye* isn't all you wanna say, huh?" I said with a little attitude.

"What do you mean?"

"I know you wanna break up with me, Myrek. We told each other we were gonna do that when I move. Since I'm probably leaving today, I guess that's the end of us. It doesn't make any sense to hold on to being a couple when I'll be in Orlando and you'll be here in Jacksonville. Plus, we're only in the ninth grade. We both should be free, right?"

Myrek was quiet. He didn't say anything; I knew this was hard for him too. But at least a part of me was happy. After all, we've been best friends for years and had tons of good memories. Growing up, York, Yancy, Myrek, and I were inseparable. I didn't care if I was a tomboy; we'd had so much fun. The three of us were gonna have a tough time gettin' by without him.

Then he broke the silence and asked, "Does it even matter if we're still boyfriend and girlfriend?"

I didn't know how to respond to his question. Of course it mattered to me. Was this a trick question or was there something deeper he wanted to get at?

"Talk to me, Myrek. I don't seem to understand what you're asking. Do you want us to break up?"

"We can break up; it's what we decided. But just because you're not my girlfriend doesn't mean I'll stop caring for you. We can turn off the words, but I can't turn off my heart. I guess what I'm trying to say is that I'll always care about you, Yasmin Peace. If you ever need me, I'll be there."

I had to cut him off. "Well, I gotta go. My dad's here."

"Okay, cool. I'll be right over to get in some last good-byes and help close up some boxes or something."

"Myrek?"

"Yeah?"

"Thank you."

"For what?"

"For being real and cool like that. I appreciate you sharing your feelings with me."

"Same here." I could tell he was smiling when we hung up the phone.

"Hey, Dad," I said as he walked into my room.

"You're not happy to see me, are you, baby girl?" I just looked away. He was trying to move me to a world I wanted no part of. "Well, come on out anyway. Your mom wants to talk to you."

"Mom wants to get on me about not being done packin' up my boxes. Can you stall her?" I asked.

He smiled and urged me. "Just come out for a second."

"All right," I said, finding nothing to smile about.

I guess this was it. Since we were being called together in the living area, it must be time to find out exactly when we'd be taking off. No way was I prepared for what our parents were about to tell us.

"Guys, your dad has talked me into not moving right now," Mom announced.

I couldn't believe my ears! I jumped out of my seat, ran over, and hugged her. "Thanks, Mom! Thank you!"

York and Yancy seemed to be in a state of shock; surprisingly, neither of them made a move.

"It's only for a couple of months," Mom explained. "We decided not to react too quickly; we want to do things the right way. We're not even married yet and we need a little more time to get things together. I'm sorry I had you kids pack up, but I just panicked. Now your dad has reassured me," she said as she walked over to him and they hugged, "he's got us and everything is gonna be okay. So we don't have to rush and leave right now."

Now it finally sunk into my brothers' heads what Mom was saying. My two counterparts gave each other a high-five and shouted in unison, "Yeah. That's what I'm talkin' about!"

I was overwhelmed with joy! All I could say was, "Can we pray? I'm so happy, guys. Can we please pray?"

"I think that's a good idea," Dad said. We all held hands and bowed our heads as he led the prayer: "Lord, I love my family and I thank You for helping me get my life together so I could be back with them. Their mom and I really want to give them a good life. We thank You for taking care of Jeff Jr. We miss him so much but we're gonna stick together so these three can please You and be successful in their lives. I just don't wanna take my kids through unnecessary changes. Their security and happiness is important to me. Although we're parents and we have to make decisions, we do take their feelings seriously. We just wanna do the right thing.

"Thank You for lovin' us and thank You for providin' a way. Lord, we can't see exactly how You're gonna work it all out for us, but You will—and that gives us peace. We love You for it. In Jesus' name, we pray. Amen."

Suddenly, there was a knock at the door. With a big smile on my face, I opened it to see Myrek standing there. "Okay, you look a little too happy to be movin'," he observed.

"We're not movin' yet! Dad talked Mom into letting us stay until school is out. Isn't that great?"

Myrek said, "Wow! That's really cool! I'm shocked and I'm glad. But I guess stranger things happen."

# Chapter 8

# Stumbler over Words

*W*ithout her admitting it, I could tell Mom was a little disappointed that Dad had decided now wasn't the perfect time to move. They were in agreement, but she'd given him a half-hug when he tried to embrace her. Then she quickly headed to her room. Yep, she was upset all right.

"Wait, wait, Mom," Yancy called her. "York and I wanna go down to Orlando and stay with Dad for spring break. Is that cool?"

"I don't care. Do whatever," she said, confirming she wasn't happy.

"All right!" my brothers yelled. Then they jetted to grab their bags.

Dad hugged me and said, "Is that okay, sweetie? I just want to spend some guy-time with the boys. When we get back next Sunday, I'd love to take you out to lunch—just you and me. Is that all right?"

"Dad, as long as I don't have to move right now, you and me are so good. Go ahead and hang out with your sons. I get to stay! Yea! Thank you, Daddy," I said as I hugged his neck. "Thank you!"

"Your mom's not happy," he said, confirming what I was feeling. "I hope she forgives me. We decided together that it would be better to move later. But she's really ready to go, so now she's sad. Take care of her for me while we're gone. Okay?"

The more I thought about it, she did need some tender loving care and attention. Mom had been under a lot of pressure and real moody the past few months. Now I understood that she was really angry over losing her job and getting deeper into debt. I'd help us all out and love on her a little extra.

My brothers took their bags that were already packed and got into the car with Dad. After they were gone and the apartment was quiet, I just laid down and took a nap. There wasn't a "Do not disturb" sign on my mom's door, but I didn't dare bother her.

A couple of hours later, I woke up to the phone ringing. It was my friend Veida calling to make up. I was happy that she called and even happier that I could give her the good news.

She was thrilled too. "I'm so glad that you don't have to move right now, Yas. I don't know how to say I'm sorry, so I guess I'll just come out and say it. I'm sorry that I was acting like such a brat!"

"It's okay," I said, realizing it was difficult for her to find the words. But since she cared about our friendship, she did find them.

"I guess I just missed my best friend. I've been a terrible friend, Yas, please forgive me."

"Just don't worry about it," I said to her.

"I do have to worry about it. I blamed you for what somebody else did."

"Well, I'll be home with my mom tonight; my brothers are

gone out of town with my dad. Maybe you can come over and spend the night so we can catch up on what's been happening the past few weeks."

"I'd like that," she said.

"Before you ask your folks, let me check with Mom first. She's been upset lately. I'm thinking she wants to hurry up and be with my dad, you know?"

"Yeah, girl, I know. If I loved a guy I wouldn't want to be away from him. Just let me know what she says. Talk to you later."

After telling Veida that I'd call her back, I knew it was time to check on my mother. We hadn't spoken since Dad and the boys left, and I really didn't know what kind of mood she was in. When I knocked on her door, I was surprised to see her up. It made me smile when I saw her dressed up all cute.

"Mom, I thought you were bummed. I mean, where are you going?"

"My girlfriend, LaDonna, invited me to her cousin's birthday party. She doesn't live too far from here, so I won't be too late."

"Well, I was wondering if Veida could spend the night."

"If it's all right with her parents, then it's all right with me. Just make sure they know I'll be out and that the boys aren't here."

"I will. Thanks, Mom."

"Sure, Yasmin."

"Mom, I'm sorry I didn't wanna hurry up and move. Thanks for not making me. A couple of months from now it'll be bad enough."

"Yasmin, life wouldn't have ended if you had to move right away. People have to do what they gotta do in this tough economy and it's not always easy. But your dad and I did talk about it and we feel that staying until the end of the school year is best. It will give us more time to get ready. I was a little salty, but I'm good now. You guys seem happy too. It'll all work out."

I couldn't think of anything to say so I just gave her a huge hug. I called Veida and told her she could come on over. And in less than thirty minutes she was at my door.

"I don't want you girls opening the door for anybody tonight. You got that, Yasmin? I don't even want you on the phone. No one needs to know you're here alone. If you're hungry, there's food in there; some popcorn, hot dogs, Ramen noodles, and stuff."

Before she could finish giving us her rules, someone was at the door. She grabbed her purse, thinking it was Miss LaDonna. But it was Miss Sandra instead. I hadn't seen her since she tricked me and took her kids. When Mom answered the door and I saw who it was, I wanted to yell out *I can't believe you're here!* Mom just stared at her with her hands on her hips. No doubt she was thinking the same thing.

My mother said, "What's up with you? What you come by here for, Sandra?"

"I just came to apologize. If you were in my situation, Yvette, you would have done the same thing."

"No, you're wrong. I wouldn't have tricked a young girl. I wouldn't have scared the whole neighborhood into thinkin' somethin' had happened to those babies. I wouldn't have done anything like that, Sandra."

"Okay, so I was wrong. That's what I came by to say. I just love my babies; that's all. Now DCF is going to be involved. I know you're related to those people who got my kids. Don't get me wrong, I'm grateful, but don't you know how bad it would feel for someone to take your kids?"

Mom responded, "The kids may be better off, Sandra. Did you ever think about that? You need to do what's best for them."

"I'm gettin' myself together. I'm fine now. I'm sober. You gotta tell the judge that. You gotta help me, Yvette. Will you help me?" Miss Sandra pleaded.

"I'll—I'll see what I can do. We'll talk later. Okay?" Mom said as she shut the door.

She couldn't even give the lady a straight answer and had stumbled over her words. I know she didn't wanna tell Miss Sandra one thing while planning to do another. It was just a hot mess. With DCF involved, what was going to happen to those kids? I was glad this was in God's hands and not mine.

❦

Veida and I were having a great time just laughing, cutting up, and being honest about how we both had treated each other. It was pretty cool to just let the words flow and not hold back the truth we felt inside. Putting myself in her shoes, I could see how she felt I had betrayed her. When I found out what was going on, I didn't give Perlicia and Asia a lot of drama or force them to break up with my brothers. So it did look like I was siding with them.

This was my opportunity to explain myself and tell her that I thought the whole thing was a big mess. I didn't think it was okay but there was no way I could tell them what to do. She understood and I was relieved.

"Well, enough about those two. I don't want the thoughts of them to ruin this great night we're having," I said.

"You know what, Yasmin? I really want us to be friends who can really trust each other. I'm so glad you're not movin' right now.

This time I'm gonna value your friendship even more. Of course, I realize Myrek is really your best friend."

"Myrek," I said, scratching my head. "I don't even know where to begin talkin' about him."

"Y'all are still together, right? We all knew that picture of you and Billy didn't mean anything. At least, I did. I put on my webpage that everybody was makin' that photo more of an issue than what it really was."

"I appreciate that, girl."

"He is a hottie, though," Veida added.

Before I could react to her comment, we heard a loud thump against the wall. It was coming from outside the apartment. She and I panicked. *What is it now?* I wondered.

"What if it's that crazy neighbor of yours? He might've been watching your mom when she left," Veida suggested. She was talking about the man who had barged his way into our place last year when I was alone.

Trying to think rationally, I said, "That guy got into trouble with the cops. He has a restraining order on him, so he can't even come around here."

"We should call the cops then," Veida replied. "*Somebody's* out there."

"Hold up. It's probably an animal or something. It'll go away. I'm just gonna look out the window."

"What if it's somethin' scary?" Veida said. I could hear the fear in her voice when she said, "Be careful."

"I'm just saying I gotta know. I'll take a peek. Turn off the lamp so they can't see me, if somebody is out there."

Once the light was off, I took a deep breath. Then we lifted up the bottom of the blinds to peek out the window.

"I can't see anything," Veida whispered.

I said, "Let's raise it a little higher."

As soon as we did that, I was surprised when we saw two girls standing by my brothers' window. When I pushed my window up a little to hear what was going on, the voices we heard sounded all too familiar. It was dark and I couldn't see Veida's face, but she and I were thinking the same thing: Asia and Perlicia were outside trying to get into my brothers' room!

"Have they been doin' this all along?" Veida asked. "Is that cool with you?"

"Wait a minute. No way; I've never known them to sneak into my brothers' room," I said, trying to adjust to what was going on.

As a matter of fact, I had no idea what they were doing out there. But I needed to find out. So I put on my shoes and told Veida, "Stay here."

"Uh-uh; I'm not gonna stay here. I want them to know that girls don't need to be sneakin' into boys' windows. No wonder they chose them over me. I would never do somethin' so stupid."

"We don't even know what's goin' on yet, Veida."

"What, are you takin' up for them?" Veida said boldly.

"Why does it have to be about taking anybody's side? Just stay here."

"Nope," she said, putting on her shoes and following behind me out the door.

When they heard us approaching, Asia and Perlicia tried to run. I called out, "Wait! Stop! We see y'all."

"Hey, Yasmin, girl," Perlicia said all fake and phony.

"She saw you at her brothers' window. So don't 'hey, girl' her," Veida spoke up, standing right beside me.

"Okay, fine," Perlicia said, stepping up to Veida's face. "What are you gonna do about it? This ain't your house anyway."

"Hey, girls!" Asia said. I noticed she was acting a little weird. For some reason she was wobbling like she couldn't stand up straight. Then she fell right into Perlicia.

Perlicia scolded her. "Stand up, girl. You can't even hold it, and you made too much noise."

"Hold what? Do you have to go to the bathroom?" I asked Asia.

Veida jabbed me in the arm and said, "This is crazy. You're supposed to be gettin' them straight, not playin' potty time."

I was curious and I needed to know. So I asked them, "Have you sneaked into my brothers' room like that before?"

"It's really none of your business," Perlicia responded. She had the nerve to be getting an attitude with me.

"Well, that's called trespassing, and I *could* call the police. I don't think you wanna be gettin' too tough with me right now," I said, standing up to my so-called friend.

Perlicia wasn't backing down. "Call the police, Yas? Come on. We're your girls and we were just havin' a good time. Don't start trippin' because 'Little Miss Perfect' is beside you, acting like she never did anything wrong."

"Yeah," Asia said in a spacey kind of way. "Don't let her spoil all the fun. I do have to use the bathroom, though. I mean, potty. Yasmin, can I come in?"

Then Asia fell into my arms and I realized that she had been drinking something. Disgusted, I turned my head away from the smell of alcohol on her breath.

Then Veida reminded me. "Your mom said you couldn't have any company." The frown on her face let me know it was a bad idea.

"She just needs to use the bathroom," I responded.

"Yeah, so just stay out of it," Perlicia sneered as she starting helping Asia toward my door.

"Wait! I didn't say she could use it!" I blurted out.

"So what, she can't?" Perlicia asked.

"You just wanna see if her brothers are in there," Veida said, shaking her head disapprovingly.

"Trust me, if her brothers were here, they would already be with us," Perlicia snapped back.

Veida looked straight at me. "That's it. If they come in, I'm leaving," she said flatly.

"Can we all just calm down, please!" I yelled. "We're supposed to be friends. We're supposed to be cool. I—I—I . . . Really! You know what I'm tryin' to say. Just get along, all right, y'all!"

Then I turned to Veida to reason with her. "I'm just gonna let them use the bathroom and that's it. Where are you gonna go? It's late. They'll be in and out. I promise."

"I just don't wanna be around them. You see how Perlicia's been gettin' smart with me and stuff," Veida said, pointing at our sassy girlfriend.

Perlicia gave Veida a very mean look as she started moving Asia toward the door. I gave Perlicia a stern look for her to leave Veida alone. Then I tugged at Veida's arm to make her go back inside. Finally, we were all in the house.

Veida sat unwillingly on the couch. I was getting ready to sit next to her when I turned just in time to notice Asia going into my room.

"There's no toilet in there," I said quickly. Then I went to lead her into the bathroom, turn on the light, and shut the door.

I found Perlicia in the kitchen, reaching for a glass. I tried to talk some sense into her. "Listen. Let's try to get along. Okay?"

"Just keep her away from me and we'll be fine," Perlica said in a salty way.

"What were y'all doin' over here? Have y'all been over here like that before? This is my house; you know I got the right to ask these questions."

"No, we haven't been over here before like this. We were just havin' a little fun. You need to loosen up yourself and have some of this wine we took from Asia's refrigerator." Perlica reached inside her jacket and pulled out a long bottle that was nearly empty.

I was totally shocked! "Oh, my goodness! What are you doing with that?"

"Calm down. Asia said her mom wouldn't even miss it," Perli-cia said coolly.

I couldn't believe they would go this far. Asia's mom would kill her if she found out Asia took that! It just made me all the more determined that they had to leave.

Standing firm, I said in serious tone, "Well, anyway, y'all just need to use the bathroom and go."

"Oh, so it's like that now? Huh, Yas? You're just gonna kick us out? You need to taste some of this, girl. You gotta enjoy life."

It was time to get her told. "Look. My mom said I couldn't have anybody else over tonight. I do want us all to be girls again. I just don't think that can be possible at the moment. Until y'all de-cide to get it together, y'all not gonna be up in my house cuttin' up. You might not wanna listen to Veida, but she's right about y'all being out of line tryin' to get through my brothers' window."

It was just the two of us and I finally had her attention. I really wanted her to hear what I was saying. "What did you think my brothers were gonna do, let y'all in and y'all would be in the room right across from my mama? And even if that could go down, and, believe me, it couldn't, what would they think of you the next day? You try to act all bad, Perlicia, but you're really not. You're not a fast girl; you want a true boyfriend.

"Yeah, York is wild around the edges and that seems appealing to you, but you want a real relationship. I'm telling you, the things you've been doin' is no way to get him. As much as you think you might know him because you've been goin' to school with him for the past few years, you really don't know him at all." I was clearly stating the facts for her.

She tried to justify her actions. "But if I don't hang with him, then he's just gonna find somebody else."

"Well, I'm telling you this even though he's my brother; if he's putting any pressure on you, then you don't need him because you'll never have real peace inside. You know this is wrong. Don't tell me you actually think you gotta drink alcohol so he'll want to hang out with you? Wow. I love you, girl, but y'all gotta stop." I just shook my head.

Without saying anything more, Perlicia had heard enough. She dashed out of the kitchen and headed to the bathroom door. "Come on, Asia, let's go!"

"I don't feel well, y'all. I can't go nowhere," Asia said from the other side of the door. She sounded weak.

All of a sudden we heard her heaving. Not once, not twice, but three times. I let out a deep sigh. This wasn't good.

Veida came to where we were talking outside the bathroom door and asked us, "Who's gonna clean up the mess in there?" Then she spoke directly to Asia, "I hope you threw up in the sink or the toilet."

"Do you really believe she's thinking about that right now?" Perlicia said angrily to her. "I am so sick and tired of you gettin' into everybody's business. You think you're so perfect. We didn't wanna hurt you. Her brothers just weren't into you anymore, Veida. They like us. And what kind of friend are you anyway? Just because they weren't into you, you got mad at us like we were supposed to have some kind of special loyalty to you. You couldn't even decide which one you wanted to be with. Just go somewhere and sit down."

"Perlicia, you better get out of my face," Veida charged back. But Perlicia got closer and closer. Then Veida pushed her and shouted, "I said get out of my face!"

But Perlicia wouldn't back down. She pushed Veida so hard that she lost her balance and fell backward.

I shouted out, "Stop, you guys! Stop right now!"

This mess was spinning way out of control—definitely out of my control. The girls wouldn't stop fighting and Asia was calling for my help.

I got sick to my stomach when I walked into the bathroom. Now I see why people aren't supposed to drink.

When I heard the sound of heavy glass crashing, I knew was in serious trouble. But when I ran to see what had happened, I learned that it wasn't an object that broke my mom's piece of furniture—it was Veida's head. The mess in the bathroom didn't compare to the blood and trauma Veida was experiencing.

"Oh, no! All I did was push her back! Oh, Veida, I'm so sorry!" Perlicia cried out.

I tried to see if my friend was moving, but she wasn't. My heart stopped. I remembered when my brother was in the fire and I didn't know if he was going to be okay. There was a horrible feeling in my stomach and now that feeling was back again. Veida was lying there very still—but she just had to be okay.

"We have to call 911!" I shouted.

"Oh, no!" Asia said as she covered her mouth in surprise. After her last round of being sick, she had made her way into the room and witnessed the horrible scene of our friend lying there on the floor.

"What did I do? Somebody help us! Is she going to be okay? I'm so sorry, Veida!" Perlicia cried as she knelt next to our friend. My tough friend was really shook up and getting all emotional.

As I dialed 911, I was crying too. Veida still wasn't moving. What was happening?

The calm voice on the line announced, "911. What is your emergency?"

"Yes, help . . . my friend—she's—," I stumbled, unable to complete my thought.

The operator responded, "Miss, I can't understand you. You have to speak clearly. What happened to your friend? Right now I need you to tell me what is going on. I can't help if you're a stumbler over words."

# Chapter 9

## Stricter than Before

*T*he paramedics couldn't get there quick enough. Asia was back in the bathroom; she was feeling sick again and moaning a lot. Perlicia stood helplessly over Veida's motionless body. As hard as I tried to keep it together, I was shaking worse than if I were in minus-ten-degree weather without a coat on. I couldn't think of anything else to do but pray.

In desperation, I prayed out loud: "Lord, please help us! You gotta help my friends. Asia keeps moaning like she's gonna die, Perlicia is afraid that Veida is dead, and I'm thinking maybe she's right. Please help us, Lord!"

As we waited for the ambulance to arrive, it seemed like forever. "Veida, please, open your eyes! Come on, girl. You're gonna make it. Wake up!" Perlicia kept screaming out.

I wanted to reach out and tell my "usually carefree" friend that Veida was going to be okay, but I just didn't know. Then it dawned on me, the last time something crazy happened at my house and I didn't call my mom right away it was so bad. Back then I got scolded for not keeping her informed. As bad as I didn't wanna tell her what was going on, I knew it would be worse if I didn't let her know.

Before I could pick up the phone and call her, I got distracted when I saw Asia crawling across the floor.

"Yasmin, help me. I don't feel good at all. Yasmin, please," Asia cried as I went over to check on her. "I think I'm having a heart attack. My chest is burning so bad," she moaned.

"You just had too much alcohol, girl," Perlicia told her. She couldn't resist the chance to take a crack at her best friend.

All of a sudden, Veida's frail voice moaned, "Ooh . . . my head. It hurts." She was coming out of it!

Perlicia and I started jumping up and down in relief. Pretty soon after that the ambulance arrived. As they examined her, I held my breath.

"Is she gonna be okay?" I blurted out, not being able to hold it any longer.

The workers proceeded to give Veida stabilizing care, attending to the big gash on her head.

"Have you called an adult?" the rescue worker asked me.

"No, sir." I remembered that I hadn't called Mom when he asked.

"Well, you're going to have to get someone on the line; a parent or guardian must be alerted immediately. You should call a responsible adult to get here as quickly as possible."

I phoned my mom. And when she answered, I couldn't find the words to say anything that made any sense. Then Veida started yelling out in pain as the paramedics were tending to her. "What's going on over there?" Mom asked.

"Mom, you have to come home now. It's not good," I said, finally able to pull myself together enough to make a reasonable sentence.

"Yasmin, you have to tell me what's wrong right now! What happened!" she ordered me.

"Mom, it's not good . . . Veida is hurt. Please, come home! Now!"

"May I speak to your mother, please?" the rescuer interrupted me. I gladly handed him the phone. "Yes, ma'am, this is Sal Freeman and I am a rescue worker with Duval County. There's been an accident at your home. You need to get here as quickly as possible. The young lady needs medical attention and we are escorting her to the emergency room. Her parent or guardian must be alerted. Please contact them immediately; one adult should travel with the young lady."

"Oh, my goodness!" She yelled loud enough for everyone in the room to hear her.

The man continued. "The emergency room staff will need authorization to administer care to the patient. The other three young ladies need adult supervision . . . Yes, ma'am, I understand." That was all he said before he hung up the phone. "Your mom is on her way. She's calling this girl's parents now."

Asia was sitting on the floor, rolled up in a ball, and rocking back and forth. She moaned as though she was in total misery.

The paramedic asked, "Is everything okay with her or do we need to take a look at her?"

"No, sir. She's fine."

He spoke with authority. "It looks like alcohol was involved here; I see the empty bottle. When teens drink alcohol, the situation can quickly get out of control—you are not ready to handle it in a responsible way. There's nothing grown-up about drinking alcohol at your age; it can put you in serious danger. I'm sure your parents have warned you about it. You should listen to them and act accordingly—that's the grown-up way. Get your friend some water and tell her to breathe in deeply. The alcohol needs to wear off before she moves around too much."

As they prepared to put Veida into the ambulance, Mrs. Hatchett phoned. Understandably, she was highly upset as she told the paramedic that she and her husband were on their way.

Veida's parents arrived in a flash. They spoke briefly with Mr. Freeman and Veida's mother rode in the ambulance with her daughter. Mr. Hatchett followed in their car. Hearing the sound of the siren as they took off was so unsettling. I couldn't help but wish that all of this was just a bad dream.

Two minutes later, Mom yelled out as she and her girlfriend came busting in the door, "Yasmin! Yasmin!"

When she saw me, she ran over and gave me a real big hug. I thought I was in trouble. It took me by surprise when she was so ecstatic to see that I was okay. But I guess I got excited too soon because when she saw that I wasn't cut, bruised, or hurt in any way, she gave me a strong slap on my backside. It made me really feel her disappointment in me, and I knew that I deserved it.

"What were y'all doin' in here and what were y'all thinkin'? Didn't I tell you, no other company over here? And you disobeyed me anyway!"

Feeling awful, I replied, "I know, Mom, but it's a long story."

"I'm listening," she said with a very serious tone.

"Miss Peace, I don't feel well," Asia spoke up. Perlicia had been trying to keep her quiet.

Perlicia had also tried to hide it, but Mom saw the bottle, picked it up, and said slowly, "Girls, I am so disappointed in you."

"But, Mom—"

"No, no buts. I let you talk your way out of so much; it's time for you to take responsibility." Holding the empty bottle, she continued talking. "This is not supposed to be in my house. I'm gonna say it in a way so that y'all will understand me. I know this wasn't here when I left home, so whoever brought it in here needs to know I don't appreciate this at all.

"I know you two girls are interested in my sons. Y'all went to the little dance together and now you think you're grown. I don't want my daughter or my sons to hang out with girls who drink. And, Asia, you ought to feel horrible; you had no business drinking alcohol and you know it. Girl, wait 'til I tell your mother. And, Perlicia, I'm disappointed in you too. Maybe this experience will knock some sense into all of you."

Then my mother reminded me of something my old Sunday school teacher had once taught us. Our youth pastor, Rev. Crane, talked about the Scripture in the book of Ephesians, chapter 6. He even had us do a role play where he divided the class into groups. Some of us in each group were parents and some were children. Each group of "parents and kids" had a different situation to act out to show both sides of what happens when kids either obey or disobey their parents.

Mom said, "You know, God is not pleased when young people disobey and do things they have no business doing. You really need to understand what the Bible says about the benefits of obeying your parents. It's for your own good. Not only will you stay away from trouble and things that can hurt you, but God has promised kids who honor their parents that they will live long and good lives. And y'all can't tell me that you don't want to have happiness and peace in your life. Well, that means there's no way around it. If you want good things to happen for you, then you've got to do what's right. And this ain't right."

"Mom, I didn't drink none of that stuff," I finally blurted out.

"The fact of the matter is that you disobeyed me by letting somebody else in this house other than Veida. As far as the alcohol goes, by lettin' your friends come over, you allowed it to be here, so you're just as guilty as the ones who drank it. Now you're gonna have to pay the price."

My eyes were filled with tears and my emotions were all over the place. I was glad Veida was gonna be okay. When I looked at Asia, she seemed to be feeling a little better; so I was glad about that too. But I was also glad that I let my girlfriends in before they could get into even more trouble. Still I was broken. And being real honest with myself, I was broken because I let my mother down once again.

For most people, this was spring break—a time of fun. However, it wasn't much of a break for me because I was on punishment. Mom reminded me constantly how disappointed she was in me, how I had disobeyed her orders, and how my friends led me into doing something wrong.

Having fun was not an option and I was getting really bored.

So I turned on the TV. Then out of the blue, there came a roar from Mom. "I didn't tell you that you could watch any TV!" she barked.

In the back of my mind I was thinking, *Well, you didn't tell me that I couldn't either.* Of course I didn't say it; I was already in enough trouble. When I went into the kitchen to get some ice cream out of the freezer, she came at me again.

"I didn't tell you that you could eat that! You're on punishment," she reminded me again.

Her point was, I shouldn't dare to assume that this was going to be spring break as usual. Being on punishment took the joy out of any break I would have. Every time I asked her for permission to do something or just started doing things I wanted to, Mom would get me straight. It felt so bad.

Then all of a sudden, she took me by surprise. "Pack up your stuff, Yasmin. We're going to visit my mother," she ordered me.

Maybe because she was mad at me, it sounded like it was a part of my punishment. I was already beating myself up over what had happened and the last thing I wanted was for her to stay mad at me. Finally, I apologized, "Mom, I'm sorry."

"I understand you're sorry, Yasmin, and I have to recognize the fact that you're a teenager. But the reality is that your friend got hurt bad and needed stitches while she was over at my house and under my watch. Even though her parents knew I was going out, I still feel responsible. I thought that I could trust my daughter to do the mature thing and honor my wishes—but you didn't. You say you're sorry, but I don't even know if you truly understand the level of trust you have broken."

When Mom had called to check on Veida, Mrs. Hatchett told

her that Veida was going to be okay. It was a pretty serious wound, but the doctor had said the glass stopped short of severing a blood vessel. Otherwise, the outcome would have been much worse.

With tears in my eyes, I said, "Mom, I don't care if you want me to stay on punishment for the rest of the break, the rest of the school year, or even all of my high school years. It still won't replace the fact that I feel horrible about what happened to Veida. I'm really sorry that I disobeyed you. I just want you to love me again."

She came over and gave me a big hug. "I still love you, Yas. I'll always love you. Just don't think for one minute I'm not gonna stay on you and punish you when you step out of line. There are consequences when you take wrong actions. When you disobey me, you leave yourself open for a lot of drama to happen. Do you get what I'm sayin'? Am I makin' sense?"

"Yes, ma'am."

"I'm sorry if I've been extra hard on you. To enjoy this life, I want you to understand that you just got to make smart choices," she continued as we got in the car.

My mom borrowed a car from her friend and we were riding down to Orlando in complete silence. Talk about punishment; it bothered me so much that she wasn't saying anything to me. I didn't dare say anything to her. The last thing I wanted was for her to go off on me again. Thankfully, she already told me that she loved me, but at the moment we weren't friends. And that bothered me.

Then too as she rubbed her brow, I noticed that she seemed extra tired. I quietly checked her out and realized that I'd had never seen so many gray hairs on her head; they were all over. And the lines on her forehead were obvious with the gloomy look she had on her face. This was scary.

"Mom, are you okay?"

"I'm just dealing with life one day at a time, that's all. Sometimes it's not a bed of roses."

She sounded so down; I just wanted to find a way to encourage her. I didn't know exactly what it was, but I could tell that she was handling a whole bunch of tough things. Maybe she was having an emotional moment over the loss of her oldest son. She could be bummed out because she never went to college and now she has to settle for lower paying jobs. She was probably upset because we're not moving to Orlando right away so that she can make up lost time with my father. It could be all of these things. And, surely, she's disappointed that somehow her daughter keeps getting it wrong.

Lately, I'd been getting in the Word of God to help me through my punishment. I really wanted to grow. *Maybe I can encourage her,* I thought.

"Mom, have you ever read the book in the Bible called Habakkuk?" She shook her head no. "Well, it's pretty interesting. It's about a person's dreams and how people get sad when things aren't coming into place quick enough."

"And what did you get from it?" she asked with curiosity.

I replied, "I'm trying to learn it from memory. Habakkuk 2:3 says, *"For the vision is yet for an appointed time, but at the end it shall speak, and not lie: though it tarry, wait for it; because it will surely come, it will not tarry."* It means that your dreams will come true. We can trust what God says about the future. Even though it may take a long time, just keep on waitin' because it will happen! So I want to say to you, Mom, I know it's a lot when you're down and it's a lot when I keep givin' you stress. But keep prayin' and keep believin'. Everything is gonna be all right."

Scratching her head with one hand and keeping the other on the steering wheel, she said, "I just hope my mom is okay. I haven't been there enough to check on her. I hope everything is okay with her."

*Whoa! I didn't even think about that!* I thought as I slapped my palm to my forehead. She was worried about Big Mama. Duh!

She continued, "Your mom is tryin' to keep it together, Yasmin. I stay on you because I want you to have a better life than me. I want you to make better choices and learn that wondering where your next paycheck is comin' from is not the life for you."

"Yeah, Mom, I know. I don't want you thinkin' I don't appreciate the life I have now. My parents are getting back together. My brother, who wanted to be tough by being in the streets, has gotten back into sports and figured out that's where his coolness comes from. His sense of self-worth has improved a lot. And then Yancy, who never wanted to be smart, is now learning that being smart can pay off because it can get you a scholarship to go to college. On top of that, he's slammin' with the sports too. For me, I've got potential to compete at state with track. And best of all, we have a mom who loves us unconditionally, even though she won't let me eat ice cream or watch TV."

Mom laughed for the first time during the car ride. Finally, with a smile on her face, she said, "Wow, you're right, Yas. I love you, girl. Thank you. Life isn't always about material things. It's about leaving this world better than we found it and winning souls for Christ. Mama wanted me to get y'all in church so y'all could get saved. Though y'all can be knuckleheads at times, I've got some good kids. So I'm strict for a reason. You're wise, Yas, and I love you so much."

We pulled into a restaurant parking lot and went in to enjoy a much needed mother-daughter meal. Finally, after a lot of struggle, the one thing I wanted was for Mom to be proud of me. Now things were good. But I knew that I had to stay on top of things so I could make her even prouder.

⋘⋙

After we finished eating, we drove straight to the nursing home. Mom prepared me for the fact that my grandmother may not remember me. We arrived to see Aunt Yvonne and Cousin Alyssa talking with the doctor. They went over the things I wasn't supposed to do. I wasn't supposed to ask her a million questions about her memory of me.

Mom and Aunt Yvonne didn't have to think I'd drill Big Mama. Even though I was bummed that maybe my grandmother couldn't remember me, I wouldn't let it show. She had given me so much throughout my life and I'd be cool just being near her. I will always remember the good times.

Mom and her sister went back to the room first. So my cousin and I waited together. I hadn't seen her since last summer when she got me into so much trouble. I was thinking she'd be salty even though we left things on a cool note. I wouldn't be surprised if she was still upset because I had told her mom where to find her. She had been mixed up with some dude, who I learned was now in jail. Thankfully, he couldn't do any more damage to young, naïve girls.

I was actually surprised when Alyssa said, "You know, I apologize for not bein' in touch, but I've been too embarrassed to tell you."

"Tell me what?" I asked, knowing she was way cooler than I'd ever be.

"That you saved me."

"What do you mean, I saved you?"

"Well, I just wanted what I wanted. Really I was mad because my mom would hardly give me the time of day. You're my little cousin, but you came down here and got all up in my business. Since you pulled my mom in, we've never been closer. I guess I was searching for attention in the wrong places. When everything came crashing down on me last summer, it turned things around for me. Thanks to you, Yasmin, all is well."

I reached over and hugged her tight. Wow, I was so shocked. I really thought she was mad at me. Real peace and joy filled my heart.

Alyssa hugged me too and went on talking. "You know how it is. Teenagers want our parents to get it, to talk to us, and to care about us. Yeah, I know they got adult problems like tryin' to pay the bills, and keepin' food on the table and clothes on our backs. And of course we want some of the latest perks too. I understand they've got a lot going on, especially single mothers."

She had even more to say, and I just listened to her. "You know, Yas, being a teen ain't easy either. If you're a girl, you're tryin' to find a guy who cares. If you're a guy, you're just tryin' to stay cool so you won't get jacked. And if you're like us, people who live in the ghetto, life for a teen ain't easy because most of the time we're practically raisin' ourselves. But don't worry; I got you, Yas. I'm glad you're movin' back here."

I couldn't smile and be happy at that. I knew she was tryin' to tell me that she would look out for me and everything would be okay. But I already had a life in Jacksonville and I didn't wanna change it. Even so, I was trying to come to terms with it and accept that this isn't just about me. For sure, it was exciting that my parents were getting back together. I had to start looking at the good going on in my life. Enjoying peace was about looking at life with the glass half-full.

Just then, Mom came out of the room with tears in her eyes. My heart sank to see my mother feeling so sad. I knew it was hard for her to see her own mom in a nursing facility. But when she held me tight and whispered, "She's waiting to see you," I smiled because she would remember me.

When I got to the room door, my aunt was coming out. She squeezed my cheeks and said, "My mom hasn't been herself in the past few months, but she's excited to see you, Yasmin! I don't know how long she's gonna remember. I'm not gonna let you stay in there too long because you might wear her out."

"Girl, get on outta here! You act like I can't hear you. Let me talk to Yasmin! I'm fine," my grandmother called out.

I let out a giggle and Aunt Yvonne shot me a stern look like *don't get sassy*. But I was reacting to all the worrying about Big Mama not remembering me—it was for nothing.

"I'm sorry," I quickly said to my aunt.

Big Mama was so glad to see me. "Come on in, Yasmin, and sit beside me. Give me a big hug, baby."

I said from my heart, "Grandma, I've missed you so much."

"Girl, I've missed myself," she jokingly said. She was always so funny and so sweet. "You know, when I have days like this I gotta make them count. I'm sittin' here with my granddaughter; my smart, sweet granddaughter. And I just want you to know that Big Mama loves you." I didn't want her to see my tears, but they couldn't help but fall.

She looked at me hard and said, "Girl, I know you're not cryin'? Don't shed no tears for me. Yeah, I got this mean old sickness that makes me not remember things, but sometimes I don't even remember that." She just chuckled at herself.

"Why, Big Mama? Why does life have to be so hard?"

Smiling she said, "Because, baby, this ain't our home. My bags are packed and I'm ready to leave."

What was she saying? Was she tellin' me that she was ready to die? Was she givin' up on the will to live? I wanted to take her by her shoulders and shake her. I wanted to say *No, don't go; we need you here.* But then she explained what she meant. She told me it was so good that God made us in His image so that we could be with Him for all eternity. She said that this life was just a stopping place on the way to being with Him.

Then Big Mama started to talk about her life. "You know, I used to enjoy feeling the breeze on my face on a bright spring day. I'd get excited when my favorite television show came on. I used to love going out with your grandfather when he was alive; he used to take me out on dates. It gave me real peace to cook meals for my family. But you know, it's all gonna fade in comparison to what I haven't seen yet—the things God has waitin' for me in glory.

"So if this life seems hard 'cause you gotta follow the rules, don't faint. Just hold on; your change is comin'. But you gotta be ready when Jesus comes. Your mama told me she's been a little hard on you. You gotta stay in line, baby, so that you make God proud. So if I give you no more advice, get all she's teachin' you. Ain't nothin' wrong with her stayin' on you. It's okay if things are stricter than before."

# Chapter 10

# Crazier
## from It

A few weeks later I was heavy into track season. I have to say it was going extremely well. Our school had made it into the final meet! My coach was awesome, and I was so glad we had battled through not wanting to work hard. He kept telling us, "You are what you do over and over again. There's no such thing as rising to the occasion; you'll only revert back to the level of training that you've reached."

He told us that he didn't come up with the idea on his own; he just put it in his own words. It just didn't sound so cool when he kept saying it while we were in the heat, sweating and training to improve. However, as we began to excel during the season, the hard work he put us through did pay off.

Another high school in Duval County had the same record as we did. And the final meet was now between the two of us. It was time for the last female event—the 400-meter dash. The problem was we were losing the track meet. It had all come down to this:

unless we win this race, it wouldn't matter how well we did all season, we weren't going to be the county champs. When all of a sudden we weren't doing so well, naturally, my team was deflated.

"I just wanna tell you guys, it's up to us now," I said to the three other girls who were running the race with me. That didn't have much effect on them.

We were hardly bosom buddies; they were upperclassmen. And they thought I was just a little freshman who didn't matter or have much to say. But, guess what? I had speed and I ran the first leg of the race. That was really a big deal because it means I had the ability to put the team out front.

I kept talking to them. "I plan to give this my all. I know we're totally bummed out because we're behind. But like Coach Hicks said, we can do it. Are y'all with me? Do you believe?"

"Those girls are fast," one of my teammates said to me. The reaction from the other two seemed like they too had already given up before we even started. I wondered, *Where did our confidence go?*

Still determined, I tried again to reason with them. "If we lose but we gave our best effort, so what?"

The girl replied, "It's okay for you to say 'so what' because you're a freshman. This is my last year and I'm tryin' to get a scholarship to a university next year."

"Well, if that's the case, let's put on a show. I'm ready to run! Remember how hard we ran all year. This is not the time to give up. We can do this."

I put my hand out, hoping the other three would put their hands on top of mine. It seemed like forever passed by and no one did. Then, finally, one of those senior girls actually placed her hand over mine and the others followed. Then we were jumpin' up and down until everybody around us thought we had lost it.

But we hadn't lost anything. Actually, we'd found the faith to believe we could win and that our coach had prepared us for this moment. After we stepped out onto the track, the man yelled "Go!" And I flew.

As the wind brushed swiftly against my face I prayed silently, *Lord, thank You for allowing me to understand that my gift is to encourage people. Being the best I can be is making folks around me be the best they can be. I wanna run real hard. It doesn't matter if we win or lose; I just wanna give it my all. And with Your help, we can win.*

The next thing I knew, I was handing off the baton—way out in front of the girls on the other team. There were tons of cheers from our track team.

Finally, on the last leg, the last girl to run showed out. And we won! Not only did we win the race, but we won the meet. Not only did we win the meet, we won in our hearts. I think all four of us understood the same thing: no matter the odds stacked against you, just as long as you try your best and don't give up, you can overcome obstacles. Altogether, it was a great feeling.

Lately, I hadn't been talking much to Billy, mainly because Myrek asked me to stay away from him. I was still catching my breath when he came over to me and said, "That was a great race. I really admire you. You're a leader; you're very cool, Yasmin."

"Thanks," I said as I gathered myself and quickly tried to walk away.

But he wasn't ready to give up. "Wait. Can we just be friends?" he asked, catching up to me.

I paused because I really didn't know what to say. I liked him.

He was cool. But I thought that if I told him yes then I would be disloyal to Myrek.

"Hey, do you mind if I steal my daughter away?" Suddenly Dad was behind us. He surprised me real good.

"Daddy!" I cried as I turned to hug him real tight. "You made it!"

"I couldn't miss my baby girl's big meet. I hear you're going to the Olympics. I just saw the reason why myself. You were awesome!"

"You came," I repeated, hugging him again. I then turned to Billy and said, "I have to go and talk to my dad, okay?"

"Yeah, yeah. It's cool," Billy said as he took off.

I grabbed Dad's hand and we walked over to the bleachers. Coach Hicks stopped us and told my dad how good I was. He went on to brag about my potential and how he couldn't wait to work with me next year. Best of all, Coach even told Dad how I could go far in track if I stuck with it.

When Coach Hicks walked away, I said, "Dad, why didn't you tell him that I wasn't going to be here next year?"

"I didn't wanna scare the man. He sounded so excited to work with you; we'll discuss it when the time comes. I wanna talk about the young man who just asked to be your friend. Why did the cat have your tongue?"

"I don't know. Myrek just thinks the boy likes me," I said in a low tone, knowing Dad would disapprove of Myrek blocking my friendships.

"Myrek is a good guy. But I told you that I think you're too young to have a boyfriend; particularly, if it comes down to standing in the way of your friendship with someone else."

I really wanted to know, so I asked him, "Do you think I can have a boyfriend and be friends with another guy at the same time?"

"Like I said, you're my little girl and I think you're still too young to talk to any boys. But you're growing up and I'm tryin' to accept it. So, yes, it's okay as long as you are honest with yourself and both guys. You have to let them know where the line is drawn and where your loyalties are. You never need to be afraid to be anybody's friend. Remember, you're a child of God. Embrace everybody."

I hugged him real tight once more. He truly blessed me by coming to my meet and he even gave me a daddy-daughter talk. I needed that because I was losing it! Dad gave me something to think about; he helped me sort out an important issue that had been bothering me. I knew Myrek had a special place in my life, but there was no reason why I couldn't be friends with Billy too. It was gonna be all good.

❦

"Don't get me wrong, I'm happy to be out of class," Asia announced. "But I really don't like going to these assemblies. What's this one for anyway?"

"Yeah, does anybody know what this is about?" I asked Perlicia. Veida was sitting in front us. It was clear, even though some time had gone by, our friendship was still strained. She didn't even turn around once to look at us, and I was pretty sure she wouldn't bother to offer any information. I wasn't happy about it but she and my other two friends were pretty cold toward each other. We weren't really talking like we used to.

"They're supposed to be talkin' to us about drugs," Veida finally blurted out to my surprise.

"Drugs? I know I don't wanna sit and listen to that," Perlicia said in protest.

"Why do they wanna talk to us about drugs?" I asked.

Perlicia pointed toward two guys walking into the gym. I thought they were just acting extra silly. They were jerking around and laughing way too hard.

"They're on drugs," Perlicia said with a matter-of-fact tone.

"They are not," I challenged her.

"They live in my neighborhood. I know who they are. There's a lot of drug activity going on at this school right now. You can be all naïve if you want to. The school is tryin' to crack down on it and catch the people who do it. Those two are gonna get caught if they don't watch it. As bad as I don't wanna hear this lecture, it's going on for real."

I just scratched my head. How could I be so naïve? How could I not know that drugs were being sold at my school? Were my eyes not open? Was I so into my books and track that I wasn't paying attention to what was apparently going on around me? Had I lost my street smarts? Exactly what was going on and why hadn't I known about it?

On the other hand, it seemed as though Perlicia was very informed. "It's not like they're just out in the hallway sellin' it. You gotta know this is an underground operation. There's big money in the game and the stakes are gettin' higher."

Veida finally turned around and said, "Yeah, my dad said the local clinics are overloaded with teens because of drug-related incidents. Either they can't handle it and pass out, or it makes them do crazy things to themselves. My parents are actually thinkin' about takin' me out of this school."

When she turned her back, Perlicia vented her frustrations on Veida. "Good, then. Go! Nobody wants your stuck-up self around anyway. What, you think it's just the people in the projects who are on drugs? Y'all rich folks actually got the money to buy the stuff. Hate to be the one to tell you—but teens in public schools, private schools, and teens everywhere in between are into drugs," she said, waving her hands all about.

Maybe we did need to hear this talk. When I looked up, a group of policemen were entering the auditorium. There were so many standing around the walls it looked like the entire police force was in our school. The room got much quieter when the students saw who was in our presence; the officers definitely caught everyone's attention.

One of the men stood up at the podium and said, "Good afternoon, I'm Officer D. J. White. We're here to talk to you today about a very serious subject. That subject is illegal drugs. You should know that drugs have infiltrated our schools today and this is a real problem. By now you are probably aware that one student from this school has already been caught selling them. So we're here to tell you two things: One, drugs are dangerous and hazardous to your health because of their addictive nature. You can expect trouble if you're involved with them. And, two, if you insist on doing it, when we catch you, you're going to wish you'd never touched the stuff."

As the officer continued his lecture, the two guys we saw earlier were still acting crazy. I looked over in their section and noticed that while everyone was being quiet and attentive, they had started balling up paper and throwing it at people. The next thing we knew a fight broke out and they were taken out.

I couldn't help but think, *How sad is that? They must be out of their minds to get into trouble with the police right here witnessing it.*

Then I recognized one of the guys; he was in my class in middle school. That boy was an A student, and now he's on drugs. I wondered, *Why? What makes people try the stuff in the first place?*

As though he had heard my thoughts, Officer White then said, "Our study shows that more people are likely to do drugs when they have friends who are using drugs. There are other reasons people take drugs. Many young people do them to try and 'fit in' with their peers; some do drugs because they are bored with their lives; some want to rebel against their parents; and others simply want to experiment with drugs.

"None of these are good reasons. If you think that drugs can be the answer to your problems, you should know that taking drugs will only bring you problems. The outcome you will experience from taking drugs is worse than any problem you might need to work out. There is always a better solution than resorting to drugs.

"Well, today there are some young people who are here to tell you from firsthand experience why you should never do drugs. We're not trying to give you a bunch of fiction here—just facts. It's their story. They're kids just like you. Listen to them and then you can decide if this lecture is really worth it or not."

The officer motioned for the first one to come up to the podium. A guy came forward shielding his left hand. He took the microphone with his right hand and said, "I was so out of it that I took a saw and cut off two of my fingers. Honestly, I didn't even feel the pain until I woke up in the hospital. That was when I wished I'd never taken the stuff." You could hear the sighs sweeping through the whole auditorium.

Next, a girl walked up and told her story. "You might want to think hard before you let somebody talk you into doing drugs. I was so high that I dared my brother to point a loaded gun at me." She pulled up her pant leg and revealed a prosthetic limb attached to her right leg. "You can see the results for yourself."

Finally, a guy who looked to be in his twenties came up and told us, "I'm on parole. I was high one night when I robbed a convenience store. The folks I was with shot and killed the clerk. Now I feel responsible for takin' away somebody's husband and father. And I have to live with that for the rest of my life. If I knew drugs would put me so far out of my mind, I never would've touched them." Then he handed the microphone back to Officer White.

"People, these are just a few stories out of many. I'm sure you have already heard stories on your own about the negative effects of drugs. I don't care what anybody tells you about how good they may make you feel, drugs are nothing to play with. They become addictive to the point where it's hard to stop even if you want to. Drugs seriously impair your judgment and you run the risk of causing serious harm to yourself and others. Overall, selling and using drugs is a crime that you will regret committing."

Officer White concluded his talk and I only hoped everybody got something from it. I sure did. Drugs. All I could think was— *no way*. It's not worth it, and I'd make sure my bothers got the point that drugs were not their friend. Hopefully, they already knew it.

❧

For the past two semesters, I had been in health class. So I was really excited to go back to P.E. The girls were outside for softball, and the coach realized he didn't have enough gloves. So he sent me inside to get more. On my way into the equipment room, I overheard some familiar voices.

Although I couldn't see them because of the rows of lockers in between us, I knew it was York and Yancy. Judging from the way they were arguing, they were having a heated conversation about something. My brothers couldn't see me, but I was glad I could definitely hear them.

". . . I'm not tryin' to hear what he's talkin' about," York was saying. "I hit it before and it didn't do nothin' bad to me. At first it makes you feel a little weird, but after a few minutes you're good to go."

Yancy spoke boldly. "So I wanna try it. Lee said he'd give us a hit for free. Can't be nothin' wrong with havin' a little taste."

"That's just stupid," Myrek said, making me proud to know him. "This boy Lee got his stuff from who? We don't even know. We might take a little hit and then all three of us could be messed up. I heard if you get a hold to a bad batch of it, your brain could easily be fried for real."

"So, what's up?" Lee walked up to the three of them and said. "Enough talk. You dudes ready to try it?"

My legs were immovable. It was as if they were stuck in cement or something. I've got pretty good grades, but it didn't take a genius to figure out what they were talking about. Lee was selling and he was trying to get the three of them to buy. I just wanted to get between them and say no no no! But I was hoping they would be smart enough and strong enough to step up to the plate and say no for themselves. So I just kept listening.

"I don't understand what the big deal is. I'm givin' y'all a free taste. I mean, what's up? Y'all tryin' to punk out or somethin'? You supposed to be the studs around here. All the older dudes are doin' it; don't we need to feel good too? Here, just take a hit. I guarantee you'll like it, for real."

Yancy started to grab it and Myrek stepped in front of him. "How do we know this stuff ain't bogus? Where you get it from, man?"

"I can't tell you my sources, dude. Plus, it's free anyways. It ain't like you gotta pay for it to try it."

"If we like it, we gotta pay you tomorrow, right?" York asked.

"I'm hopin' y'all will pay me right now if you want some more. You gon' wanna hit this again tonight, trust me. This stuff'll make you have no cares, no problems, no worries," Lee said, selling them a bunch of lies.

"Who said we got problems?" York said with a defensive attitude.

Lee just smirked. "Come on, man. Y'all are three punk wannabes, livin' in a tore-up neighborhood and goin' to a broke-down school. Dudes around here had respect when they had a leader, but now he's locked up. It's a couple of cats around here sellin' on their own and y'all could be in the business too. But if you hook up with my man, ya'll have protection."

"What you sayin', man? If we take some of your stuff, we're initiated in a gang or somethin'?" York asked. "Naw, man. That's all right. We can protect ourselves. We don't need your stuff."

"Oh, so it's like that?" Lee taunted as he struck a match. He took a puff and blew the smoke in York's face. York charged at him. Lee just started laughing. "Man, that's all you got? You can't hurt me. None of y'all are all that . . . hit this and it can take you to another level."

I couldn't believe Lee actually did that! Didn't he hear them say they weren't interested? Why was he still pressuring them? But as I looked over at them, it seemed even after they had said no, for some reason they were still entertaining the idea.

*We need to get in the Word,* I thought. God was the only One who could make us feel higher than we could ever physically be. But my brothers weren't acting like they knew that and my boyfriend wasn't either. They were listening to this nut and it was making me so sick.

But I had to decide something quickly. My coach would be looking for me; it was almost time to play the softball game. Yet I couldn't leave now; there was so much at stake here.

"So what's it gonna be? Y'all down or not? I got other clients to deal with."

The three of them huddled together like they actually had to think it over! What was wrong with them? Was I going to have to beat all three of them up to knock some sense into them?

"All I'm sayin' is, take a little hit. If you don't like it, then I'll go on 'bout my business. You know you wanna; you just need to stop bein' wimps and try some. 'Cause if you don't, you just might be sorry," Lee said, not letting up.

"Man, are you threatenin' us?" Myrek stepped up to Lee.

Then Yancy started to cave. "If takin' a hit will make him leave us alone, then I'll do it. Anyway, who knows, I might like it."

I wanted to scream! I couldn't believe the three of them were putting up with all of this. If they tried it, didn't they know it could mess them up? Lee was already high and out of his mind. They had heard the officer say taking drugs would make you do strange things. They already had enough issues just trying to stay out of trouble—getting involved with drugs could only make them crazier from it.

# Chapter 11

## Supporter of Truth

As I saw the white object with smoke coming from one end as it passed from Lee to Yancy, I dashed across to the locker room faster than I ever had in any of my track meets.

"Yancy! What are you doing?" I said in a loud voice as I reached for the object and snatched it out of my brother's grasp.

"Yas, what are you doin' in here? We got this," Yancy said to me. He wasn't happy with me intervening.

York came up behind me and pulled me back. "Yeah, Sis, you don't need to be around this."

Myrek came to my other side and said, "Yeah, you don't need to be here. You'd better go on to class."

I wanted to give all three of them a piece of my mind and truly let them know what I thought of their stupidity. How dare they question me? I was not the one about to get caught with drugs in my hand. Actually, I was! This was insane!

Then Lee took it from me; I gladly released it. He said to

Myrek, "If you can't handle your girlfriend, my brother sure would like to."

Why did he even go there? Myrek shoved him hard in the chest. They definitely didn't need to start fighting.

As he put out the smoke, Lee went on teasing, "What, you can't take the truth, little man? She comin' all up in here tellin' y'all what y'all can't do. I figured you dudes were just some little punks. You ain't ready for this."

"Please, just leave it alone," I said to Myrek. But I could tell by his expression that he was getting more and more aggravated. He gave me a look that let me know I was too deep into his business.

Lee got loud in my face, telling me that I wasn't invited to their meeting and I should stay out of it. So I got loud right back with him. I wasn't trying to be big and bad because I had my brothers and boyfriend behind me. I was just mad that he was at our school thinking he could ruin people's lives with dope—and I told him so.

"Man, back up off my sister," York said, defending me.

"Hey, calm down. Keep it down," Yancy said.

But Lee's behavior changed instantly as though he could see someone was coming up behind us. He took advantage of the situation, and suddenly he just fell into me.

"Get off of me!" I yelled at him.

I didn't know what he was doing, but he was sweaty and it felt yucky. Trying to shake that filthy feeling off of me, I was startled when I turned around and looked into the face of our principal, Dr. Taft. He was known to be super mean and no one wanted to mess with him. He cut no kid any slack.

"What is happening here? Which one of you has been smoking drugs?" Dr. Taft sternly questioned as he looked every one of us up and down.

"It wasn't me. I'm on my way to class, sir," Lee said, trying to sound like the model student.

"No, he's not going to class. He's trying to get these guys to—" Before I could finish my sentence, York kneed me in the leg.

"Stay out of it," York mumbled under his breath.

Lee cut in and said, "No, let her talk. What were you about to say? I'm tryin' to get people to do what? I'm tryin' to go to class and you're tryin' to sell me drugs. That's what's happening."

"What?" I said shocked. I couldn't believe he just lied like that.

Then York echoed me saying, "What?"

About the same time, Yancy said, "What?"

Myrek cut to the real truth when he said, "No, don't even lie!"

But the principal gave the right response when he said, "Son, I find that hard to believe."

"Oh, so just because she gotta cute face, you're not gonna question her? Of course these three guys aren't gonna snitch on her; they're her boys. You should check her and make her empty her pockets."

Then I spoke up. "There's no need for me to empty my pockets because there's nothing in my pockets." I sounded so gullible; I fell right into Lee's trap.

Little did I know that when he bumped into me, he had put something in my jacket. As soon as I turned my pocket inside out, there was a packet of white powder and three badly rolled joints. As I grabbed them, I exclaimed, "Oh, my goodness! Sir, I didn't put these in here!"

"Oh, so you got it on you, but you didn't put that in your

pocket?" Lee interrupted. "Again, sir, they're not gonna say she did anything. They're her family. I was on my way to class, just mindin' my own business. I got a lot out of the assembly today; drugs aren't the way to go. You see she got it on her; you're not gonna let her pass, are you?" He was trying hard to sound convincing.

Dr. Taft didn't even respond. He simply gave an order. "All of you, go to my office now."

"But I didn't do anything. He planted these on me," I said defensively.

I couldn't ask him to take them to the lab and get them tested because I had touched them. This was horrible. How could I prove my innocence? Tears just welled-up in my eyes. I couldn't even begin to understand why this was happening to me. It looked like I was the one smuggling drugs inside the school. As we sat in the waiting room, the principal held a meeting in his office with the two assistant principals, some other faculty members, and two of the police officers who were still in the building. I knew I was in serious trouble.

Whether it could ever be proven that this was my fault or not, from now on, they would always look at me with suspicion. Just because I tried to help my brothers and my friend, I was being framed. How unfair was this?

As we waited for what seemed like forever, my brothers and Myrek were trying to talk to me, but I just wanted them to be quiet so that I could think. If they had gone on about their business and told Lee to get lost, there would have been no need to help them out and end up getting myself in trouble. Now I was the one who had to defend myself. Lee was a jerk and the last thing my mother needed was to get a call about me selling drugs in school. Someway, somehow it was going to be revealed that the fictitious story he had told was just that.

*Lord,* I prayed to myself, *I'm asking You again to help me. I know it was right for me to try and help my brothers, but now I can't even help myself. Where is the justice in all this?*

༄

I had been in such a good place lately; I was thinking positively about my life. Things had changed at home and I was getting the chance to finish out the rest of the year at my school. Then this had to happen. Could it get any worse?

Myrek was fidgeting and asked permission to use the restroom.

When he got up, York slid over next to me and tried to reassure me. "Ain't no need to be upset, Sis. All the evidence is going to prove you didn't have nothin' to do with this. I'll take the rap before I let you fall."

I just looked at him and shook my head. He didn't even get it. I didn't want any of us to get into trouble. We'd had our share of down times. It was the Peace family's turn to be on the upswing. Someway, somehow, I believed in my soul that God was gonna see me through this. Yes, I felt lied on and unjustly accused at the moment. But then I remembered that God said He would never leave me or give up on me.

I took comfort in that assurance and said to York, "I'm gonna be okay."

"But, Yas, you're cryin'. It's not cool."

"It's just a few tears; I couldn't hold them back. But I'm all right."

After about thirty minutes, they called Lee in first and questioned him. The fact that they would even listen to him made me even more upset. There was no telling what fibs he was saying to keep himself out of trouble. And when he came out of the room wearing a sly grin as if he'd won, Yancy jumped all over him.

"Why you gon' lie like that? Why would you pin all of this on my sister like that? Tell the truth! Tell the truth, now!"

"All right, young man, calm down," the principal said. "I need all three of you in my office now. I've already notified your mother; this is serious business."

"You're gonna talk to the three of them together?" Lee asked in protest. He was probably thinking we'd have a stronger case if we talked together.

"Yes, that's the way we're going to do it, young man. Now sit down."

Just as we were about to step inside the office, someone came into the waiting room. "Hold up, hold up," the voice from behind us said. When we turned around, it was Myrek. And Veida was with him.

Dr. Taft addressed them. "This is a closed meeting, young lady. Myrek, have a seat; we'll talk to you next. We want to hear from the triplets first."

"But please, sir, you have to hear what this guy has to say first," Veida cautiously responded to Dr. Taft.

Strangely enough, she wasn't talking about Myrek. The two of them stepped aside and there stood Lee's twin, Billy, with a very cold stare on his face. He looked over at his brother and said, "How could you do this?"

"Wait, you don't know anything and you better keep yo' mouth shut," Lee demanded.

Billy turned to the principal and declared, "Sir, I can tell you that Yasmin Peace had nothing to do with those drugs. I know it because my brother is the one selling drugs at this school. And, besides, he has a record of being expelled from school in the past for the same thing."

"What exactly do you mean, young man?" the principal asked.

"If you check our records, you'll see it's the reason we had to transfer to this school."

"Billy, you punk . . . I ain't goin' back to no juvie for this!" Lee yelled out.

"And I ain't gonna let you mess up people's lives when they haven't done anything wrong. You've tried this before. The only reason I didn't report you before now is because I was hoping you had given it up. With all we've been through, I thought you'd be finished with that stuff. But I guess I was wrong. Lee, I don't even live with my mom and dad since they broke up because of your crazy ways. No more." Then Billy just broke down and cried. I could hear the pain in his voice; he was hurting bad.

Lee got in his brother's face and said, "Blood is supposed to be thicker than water, Billy. How could you do this to me?"

Dr. Taft interrupted and asked Billy, "Where is he getting this stuff from, son?"

He was trying hard to pull himself together when he answered, "I'm not sure; probably from the same people back in Pensacola."

The officers didn't waste any time. It was tough to watch them seize Lee, handcuff him, and take him away. But Billy was unmoved by seeing his brother's resistance. I guess he was used to this kind of drama.

The principal cleared me from all wrongdoing and dismissed

us all back to class. I'm sure my gym teacher had probably heard about the incident by now, but I was given a pass to give him the next day.

Myrek and my brothers got passes too. They all slapped hands and I got a huge hug from Veida.

I could tell that my brothers and my boyfriend were all relieved; they had learned that it's not cool to get into dangerous situations like this.

York said, "Man! That was a close call!"

I responded with a warning to them all, "I hope y'all know how blessed you are. God gave you another chance. Please don't try anything like that again. It's not worth it. Don't even think about it; you got that?"

Yancy just said, "Whew, Sis, you don't have to worry about me. I get it. There's no way I could face Mom and Dad if they had to come and rescue us from jail!"

Then Myrek did something I was very glad to see. He went over to Billy and said, "Man, thanks. I know I've been actin' mad about you and Yasmin's friendship. But I see now—you got her back. Thanks for lookin' out."

"It's cool, man. If she was my girl, I'd be like you too," Billy said.

My brothers joined Myrek and Billy but they had no words. Billy made the first gesture by holding out his hand. They shook hands and made a new friend that very moment.

Then it was my turn. All I could say to Billy was, "Thank you." He nodded and smiled and just walked out. I knew he would be hurting for a while. After all, Lee was his brother. I would keep them both lifted in prayer. God answered mine and I knew He would be there for them too.

I was glad this situation was resolved so we wouldn't get yelled at when we get home. After all, my brothers had learned a good lesson and so did I. They had come real close to getting into big trouble just because they had thought about getting involved with drugs.

When I stepped out into the hallway, I was so overwhelmed with relief. We could have gotten into serious trouble; we could have ended up in juvie just like Lee. God is so good. What a cool feeling. It was such a feeling of peace.

Sitting in class on Sunday, I was really sorry I had missed last week. We were watching the end of the animated film *Joseph: King of Dreams*. Honestly, at first I thought it was going to be corny since it was a cartoon. A few minutes later, though, I was really impressed by the song "Better Than I" from the scene where Joseph was in jail.

For those of us who weren't in class the week before, Mrs. Newman gave us some background. She told us about how Joseph had gone through a lot. He'd been sold into slavery by his brothers, falsely accused by the king's wife, and thrown into prison. Just one thing after another had happened to this guy. Then when he was at his wit's end, wondering if God had forgotten him, God promoted him and made Joseph a success. He realized that, throughout all of his troubles, God was with him the whole time. Joseph's story helped me realize that my life isn't just about me, it's all about God.

Mrs. Newman came over to me. "Are you okay, Yasmin?" I didn't even realize a tear had trickled from my eye.

"Yes. I'm just so full."

"What do you mean?" she asked.

"I just feel so good right now. I mean, I still miss my brother Jeff. I'm still not happy with my parents' decision to move me away soon. I wish my mom had a job. And I still wish we had more material things. I wish when things go wrong people didn't look at me or my family as the cause. But no matter what I wish for—God knows what's best. And if I rest in God's hands and get excited about Him, then I guess that's where my true peace and happiness comes from."

To my surprise, the whole class applauded. It was a moment I would never forget. I was learning how to let go; it wasn't necessary for me to know the reason for everything. Just accepting whatever God supplies because He knows what is best—that's what God expects me to do. If He leads the way, I'll be more than okay. There's no sadness in following Christ—only true peace and joy.

Then Mrs. Newman said, "Okay, class, I'm so impressed about the story of Joseph. He was a good man who believed in honor, integrity, and truth. I've often heard it said in my lifetime that bad triumphs over good. But I don't want you to think there is truth in that—because it's not. We are taught in this life that winning is best. But you should know that what God sees as victory doesn't necessarily look like the world's idea of victory."

One of the classmates called out, "Wait, I'm confused."

"Well, basically what I'm saying is, when your ways please God, others may not be pleased with you. But when you're doing the right thing, trust Him and know that He'll make a way for you to succeed."

As we watched the rest of the film, it was so exciting to see Joseph triumph in his life. His dreams came true, he became the ruler of Egypt, and God used him to save His people. I didn't know how God was going to use me, but I was ready, willing, and able. Whatever He brought me to He would bring me through. And knowing He would never leave me is what having peace in this world is all about—and that gave me cause to smile.

So what if we don't have the biggest house. We have love. So what if my mom doesn't have a job right now. At least I have a mother. So what if we're moving to Orlando. At least my parents are together again. So what if I have to leave Myrek. I'd learned what it's like being in a relationship with a boy. *Yep, God is taking care of me,* I thought with a smile.

When I walked out of Sunday school class, my teacher called me back. "I just want to let you know that I'm so proud of you. I know you're moving soon, but I want to remind you that you're a remarkable young lady—a girl after God's own heart. Keep following Him and you'll go far. Remember, I'm just a phone call away."

"Thank you, Mrs. Newman," I replied. "You know, getting through the eighth grade was the toughest year of my life. My family was shattered into pieces and I didn't think I would ever be whole again. You helped me find God. You helped me find me. Thank you. I won't forget you and I'm going to write you."

"You'd better," she said to me as we hugged.

Just as I had joy in my spirit and a feeling of peace, I walked out into the hallway to see my uncle and aunt having a somber moment. I went up to them. "What's wrong? What's going on?"

"Everything's okay," Uncle John said to me. "Everything's good."

"No. It's not okay," Aunt Lucinda spoke with sadness. I could hear the pain in her voice. "She wants the babies and we're going to give them back to her. We're not going to take those babies through a court fight and mess up their lives. It breaks my heart . . . I just thought they were going to be ours, that's all."

"I know. I know," my uncle said to her as he held her tight. "It's all gonna work out, Lu. Don't worry. We'll ask for visitation rights. And we still got our little Angel."

"I know," she said as they walked off consoling each other.

As I watched them walk away, my uncle mouthed to me, *"She's gonna be okay."* My heart broke for them. As much as I wanted to ask God why this was happening to them, I immediately thought back to the story about Joseph and the song that had spoken to my heart.

All I could think was: *God knows best.* Right away, I had to start practicing what I'd just learned in church. I had to let go of wanting to always know why. My aunt and uncle were doing what they needed and I was going to be behind them, helping them stay on their path—and being a supporter of truth.

# Chapter 12

## Brighter Days Come

The month of May was here and the reality that I would be moving from my comfort zone in just a couple of weeks gave me an eerie feeling. But I had to admit that I'd learned so much over the past six months. I was now at peace with the fact that we were going to move. My new motto is: "Give more than you take."

So when I saw Mom in the kitchen packing dishes, I said, "Can I help? Just tell me what you need me to do and I'm on it. I know you have a specific order on how you want everything boxed up and I don't wanna mess it up."

"You wanna help?" Mom looked up and said. "You mean, without pouting lips and a grudging attitude? You wanna help, for real? I'm must be dreamin'."

"No, Mom, you're awake. For real, I wanna help. And I'm sorry I was being such a sour girl about leaving. Our family needs to be together, and if we have to move so you can have more opportunities to get a good job—then I'm all for it."

She got off her knees and gave me a hug. "Thanks, Yasmin. I'm sorry. I know it can be tough to move while you're in high school, but—"

Cutting her off, I said, "No, Mom, it's gonna be okay. I'll be okay. Wait, I am okay!"

"I'm so proud of you, Yasmin. Thanks again."

Hearing those words from my mother made me feel like I was on top of the world. All I could do was smile. As we packed, we played an album by Marvin Sapp. When the song called "Praise Him in Advance" came on, Mom was full of praise. She started shouting, "Oh, I ain't got a job and I don't know where I'm gonna find one, but God is good! He's got my baby in here sayin' she's ready to help us move. Oh, God can do anything but fail. Praise God! We love You, Lord!"

Then she got up and danced around. I joined her as I listened to the words: *I've had my share of ups and downs.* It made me think about being in the eighth grade when I didn't have any friends at all. It seemed like I had nothing but problems.

Mom kept on praising God: "Yes, things have been a little rocky with the three I have. But I know deep down they've got my back. Just like the song says, *God came and spoke these words to me, praise will confuse the enemy.*

That made me go over and turn the music down. I said to my mother, "Praise can confuse the enemy? Mom, what does that mean?"

"Oh, girl, it's so good. See, when you're down and people know it, they don't expect you to have a smile. And when you ain't got nothin', people don't expect you to act like you've got riches on the inside. When you're on your last leg, people don't expect you to act like you're still in the race. And when people don't see the result of their prayers right away, most of them don't keep praying and most of them don't thank God for what they do have. They just don't understand—it's not about what God is doin' for us—it's about who He is.

"Yas, I've been thinking about what you shared with me on the way to see Big Mama. You know, what you learned from the Bible about trusting God and having peace while we wait on Him to work things out. So I've been praising God for weeks, hoping you guys won't hate your mom for movin' you. I've been trusting God to keep us together even though the Enemy wanted to tear our family apart. And then you come strolling in here sayin' you're okay and we're gonna be okay. God is good, Yas! Lord, I thank You!" she shouted as she danced some more.

I turned the music back up and just enjoyed the moment. I didn't know if I'd like my new school or what friends I'd have, but I knew God could take care of me. Suddenly our praise time was interrupted as we heard a banging on the door as if someone was trying to break it down or something. It startled both of us.

"Who is that?" Mom said to the person on the other side. She was almost screaming at them, "You better have a good reason for bangin' on my door like you the police."

When she opened it up, it was Miss Sandra and her kids. Those little children were crying so hard. Randi wrapped her arms around me and hugged me tight like she didn't want to let me go, and Dante's little nose was running nonstop. He grabbed my mother's leg and just clung to it.

"Sandra, what's going on? Talk to me!" Mom demanded.

Miss Sandra just lost it. "I—I—I just can't do it," she said as her whole body shook. "I tried not to . . . I just wanted to ease my mind. I needed to take the edge off of being a mom again because it's a lot. I forgot about gettin' up early in the mornin' and givin' them breakfast. It's just too much . . . I thought I could do it, but I can't do this . . . you gotta take them, Yvette! You gotta give them back to your relative, your uncle, whoever. I'll sign whatever you need me to. I just can't do it! Okay?"

"Are you sure this is what you want? Do you wanna say bye to the kids?" Mom tried to gently push Dante toward his mother and he started screaming louder, clearly not wanting to get close to her.

Randi tugged on my T-shirt. When I bent down to her she said, "My mommy's friend came in and said we were bein' too loud. Then Mommy wouldn't stop hittin' Dante too hard with the belt on his back. It was bleedin' real bad, Yasmin." My mother lifted up the little boy's shirt and saw the open wound.

Miss Sandra cried, "I'm so sorry. You know I wasn't in my right mind! I wouldn't hurt him like that! It's just . . . right now . . . I don't think I'm right for them. One day I pray they understand. Yvette, you're gonna help them to take care of my babies, right?"

Mom nodded and Miss Sandra took off in a hurry. Quickly, my mother called Uncle John. And it seemed like before we could blink, he and his wife were over to the house with Angel. Immediately, when they saw their foster parents, the crying and frowns that the kids had when they first came turned to laughter and smiles. It was amazing.

Aunt Lucinda said, "I never thought we would get them back, and I certainly didn't want them back this way. But we'll be good stewards of this treasure. God's given us these three babies to raise,

John, what a beautiful gift! What a glorious day! Just look at our family." She was beaming with joy. Finally, they could enjoy some peace and be a real family.

As much as I like to see the sun shining bright in the sky and watching the stars twinkle at night (and I had to admit that thinking about Myrek's cute face was cool too), seeing this family all together and happy was a special moment. I would treasure it for the rest of my life. Mom was right. God is good!

"I can't believe your mom's lettin' you have a set. And she's lettin' us come too," Perlicia said about my little going away party.

I replied, "It's the last day of school, two days before moving day. This is our good-bye party and she and Dad are both here. It's just a few people to help us celebrate."

"I actually can't believe she's allowing us back over here," Asia said, recalling the drama from several weeks back. "But she don't have to worry because I'll never drink again."

"I heard that," Mom came from behind us and voiced. "Y'all are good girls and you've learned your lessons. I talked to both of your moms and I'm glad you got some discipline. Y'all are too young to be drinkin' alcohol. Besides, good friends are hard to come by. Yasmin didn't do what I told her to, but the more I thought on it, I'm sorta glad y'all were in the house if you were that messed up. Being out in the streets, who knows what kind of trouble y'all might've gotten into. I'm just happy you learned a good lesson."

"Yes, ma'am. Yes, ma'am. Nope, never drinkin' again," Perlicia said almost sarcastically. She could tell from the look I gave her that

I wasn't amused. Then she toned it down, and said, "I'm serious, Mrs. P."

"You better be," Mom said to her.

Sadly, I had to report, "My mom did tell Veida's dad that y'all were gonna be over. So I doubt if she'll come."

Right away Perlicia said, "Excuse me," and then walked over to where my brothers were talking.

Asia followed behind her. It was like they didn't even care how upset I was about Veida not being with us. But they were my girls too and they were here to say good-bye to me, so I tried not to dwell on what I didn't have. I needed to enjoy my friends' company. As tough as they were, they were at my house and this could be the last time we'd be together.

Then Myrek came up to me and reached for my hand as he said half-jokingly, "Oh, I'd better let go. Your dad's in the house."

"You're silly," I told him.

He gently touched my hair and said, "Yasmin Peace."

"Yes?" I answered, looking intensely at my best friend.

Myrek went on, saying, "I watched you change before my very eyes. I never thought I'd like girls, ever, until the first day of eighth grade when you went from being my best buddy to being the girl of my dreams."

"You *are* silly. Stop it," I said as I tried to keep from blushing.

"I know we agreed to the 'not staying together thing' after you left, and I'm cool with it, if you are."

"Yeah, yeah," I said to him. I didn't want him to feel pressured to communicate with me while we were in two different cities.

"But I'm just thinking . . . you're about to leave and I still want you to be my girl . . . and I don't know . . . what do you think? Should we break up?" he asked.

"Hold that thought," I said before dashing to the kitchen to find my mother. "Mom, can I go outside with Myrek real quick? We're just gonna step outside for a minute. I just need some privacy to tell him bye. Is that okay?"

"Yeah, it's fine. Just come right back in," she said as she looked at my dad. That was her sign for me not to act too grown.

"You didn't ask me," Dad spoke up. He was helping her fry some chicken.

"I wonder why, Daddy," I replied, teasing him as I shrugged my shoulders. I looked around the messy kitchen with several boxes now reopened. "I can't believe you just didn't pick up a box of chicken. Besides, Mom, you told us that we weren't gonna use any of the appliances because you didn't wanna wash them down again before we leave."

She just looked at my dad again and smiled. "You better hurry up if you want a minute outside; I'm counting—"

Dad cut in and started teasing me. "One . . . two . . . oops, time's up, you can't go out."

"Dad!" I screamed playfully and scurried on out of the kitchen.

"Jeff," Mom said as she lovingly hit him in the side.

When I got back to him, Myrek sounded nervous. "I scared you away, huh?"

"Oh, no. Come on," I replied, taking him by the hand. Leading him out and shutting the front door, I looked up at the night sky. "I'd be honored to be your girlfriend as long as you promise to tell me if things change on your end, Myrek. I don't want you to feel obligated to be with me."

"Cool. And you're gonna do the same?" he asked. I nodded and he took my chin, tilted my head, and kissed me gently. As the wind blew softly, I felt so free. If I knew one thing for sure, I knew me and Myrek would always be cool.

Suddenly, a car drove up, shining its bright headlights on us. We quickly pulled apart. Veida jumped out of the car and ran toward us. She didn't waste any time handing me a very large present.

Surprised to see her and the gift, I asked, "What is this?"

"I couldn't let you leave without sayin' good-bye, Yas."

"I thought you weren't gonna come because—"

She stopped me short. "Nope," Veida responded. "Perlicia and Asia called and talked to my dad and asked him if I could come."

"Wow. Can I talk to her alone please, Myrek?" I was so surprised when I heard that.

"Yeah, sure." He kissed me on the cheek and went inside.

Veida commented, "Hey, I thought y'all were supposed to break up."

"Did the whole school know my business?" I asked.

"No, I'm just sayin'. We're not gonna stop being best girlfriends because you're movin', are we?"

"No, we're not," I said, hugging her tight. I was so glad to see her after all.

"Good. I wanted to tell you about a guy I met; we're really just cool friends. But he wanted to come and say good-bye to you too, if it's all right with your parents. And I did tell my father that a new friend of mine was comin' over. Dad said that he would wait for me in the car; he's got some calls to make."

"You mean, you—like a guy that's not one of the three guys in my house?" I asked, laughing at the very thought.

"So what are you tryin' to say?" she joked.

"No, just kiddin', who is it?"

"It's Billy. I hope you're okay with that."

I got excited and wide-eyed. "Yeah, girl, Billy is cool."

"I've been feelin' so bad for him since his brother is gone," she said.

I could hear the care and concern in her voice. "I thought Billy was movin' back home," I stated.

"Nope. He decided to stay with his grandparents and I'm sorta glad. He's a really nice guy."

About ten minutes later, Billy showed up. Myrek and my brothers were real cool with him. It was kinda weird. There was a strong sense of peace all around us. The guys were forming a tight bond and we girls were getting ours back. The only problem was— the Peace family was about to move. But, again, I couldn't let my mind focus on a couple of days from now. I had to enjoy the moment and that's exactly what I did. The eight of us played fun card games as Mom and Dad looked on happily.

"So . . . maybe we should tell the kids now, honey. What do you think?" We heard Mom and Dad talking in the hallway. "I mean, they got these great friends and all. Everybody's gettin' a little sad; they're thinkin' the party's gonna be over soon. Maybe we should tell them."

"Yeah, maybe we should," Dad said as he held her tight in his arms.

"What are they talkin' about?" York looked up from the cards he was holding. Then, as though he got some kind of revelation, he said to us, "I know y'all can see they're ready to get married."

"We can hear, you know" Dad said as they both entered the family area. "But you are right, Son."

"For real, Pops, what's up?" Yancy exclaimed. The excitement was spreading quickly.

Then Mom announced, "My old job called and they want to hire me back. They're givin' me a raise and a company car."

"What!" Veida chimed in. "So that means y'all get to stay?"

Before anyone could answer her, York stood up and added, "And what about the marriage thing?" I could tell he was anxious to know; we all were. "I know I never brought it up or whatever, but I do want to live with both my mom and pops. What's up with that, Dad?"

"Well, it's like this. I successfully completed my probation and your uncle got me a full-time job with a trucking company up here. I'll be on the road a lot, but my main base will be here in Jacksonville."

"Then we don't have to move? What about Big Mama?" I asked. I was getting more excited by the minute.

"She's doin' good and we'll visit her every chance we get. My sister has moved her to a new facility that's much better. With both your dad and me workin', I'll be able to send them money to help take care of her." That all sounded great, then Mom said something really funny. "Now, if y'all just *wanna* move, then we can throw all of our stuff into a truck and be on our way."

"No no no!" everybody in the room yelled.

Myrek looked at me and said, "You don't have to move. So now's your chance if you wanna break up."

"He can't let you be single and available like that," Billy warned.

Myrek frowned. He knew Billy used to like me a lot. Well, now that was changing. I had to set the record straight so this new friendship we were all forming could last.

I leaned over to Myrek and said, "Don't worry; if you haven't noticed, I think Mr. Billy's already taken." Just to make sure he got my message, I nodded in Veida's direction.

Before anybody else could say a word, just then, Mom spoke up, "Veida, I think your dad is ready to go. He's honking." She was pointing toward the window.

When she stood up to go, Veida sounded happy. "It's okay for me to leave now. My girl is not going anywhere. Thanks, Mrs. Peace. Bye, everybody!" She waved as she closed the door.

⁂

Two days later when we were supposed to be on the road moving to another city, we were in the Jacksonville Municipal Court instead. There were two very special reasons. First of all, my parents got remarried! Yea! Mom even made a joke about being glad that she didn't have to change her last name.

After the ceremony, we went downstairs to the family court where my uncle and aunt became permanent legal guardians of the two kids. The judge told them that he would reopen the case in six months, and they could move toward adoption if that's what they wanted to do. They were beaming with joy and we were all happy for them.

Later on while we were eating our celebration dinner, York made a comment and Dad had to straighten him out. "Now all we gotta do is move outta the projects and we'll really have it goin' on."

He looked at York and said, "Son, we got it goin' on now. My family is together, my kids are on track in school, and my wife and me are both makin' a living. There's nothing wrong with living in the projects; it's not a bad thing. Actually, it's making us stronger. We're gonna save up some money and be smart about this thing. First, we're gonna get ourselves out of this debt, and when we've reached that goal, then we'll move on up. But more than anything, we want you three to know that we love you and we're here for you. And if we trust in God, life never has to get so bad that we can't be content right where we are."

"I hear you, Pops," York said. "I have peace in knowing Jeff Jr. is with God. But I also know suicide is not the way. Goin' through changes and not havin' everything together has led me to the One who has it all. Now I know, if God can bring you back to us, He can do anything. Dad, we're gonna be okay."

Mom hugged Yancy and me and we watched my tough brother melt into our dad's arms. I had done a lot of growing up in the last two years. We lost a brother, but gained a family that is whole. My parents were together and my brothers weren't fighting anymore. I had given up my tough, boyish ways but had come into my own womanhood. Now I even know what being a friend and having good girlfriends is like. I learned that I have to trust God daily because He knows what's best. And I know it's because His ways are higher than mine.

Finally, after months of crying, months of anguish, and months of pain—I have found faith, hope, joy, and love. And just like my last name, I was finally enjoying true peace, knowing that even though this is a great moment—when you trust God—brighter days come.

# Acknowledgments

*I* just turned the big 4-0. Whew! If I'm blessed with the life span of my grandmothers I'm at the halfway point in my life. Looking back I've had some highs and some lows. The one constant I've learned is that in order to enjoy true peace you must see everything from a godly perspective.

We all want much in this life. Much love, much money, much friends, just much. But God's Word says He'll supply our needs. Doesn't say He gives us our wants. Young people, you'll be much happier in this life when you understand God loves you most and He will make sure you're taken care of. Even in the storms of your life, He can give you rest.

Peace is a mind-set you can pray for. Be ready to look at the good side of every situation. There is much I'd like to do in this world in service for my Lord. However, I know much will be out of my control. Therefore, if I seek God first, everything else will be okay. There is no way to have true peace without God. He is the only way to happiness. Get wrapped up in Jesus and you'll have peace. Here is a thank you for all those who help me to understand that my writing brings peace to many.

For my family, parents Dr. Franklin and Shirley Perry, Sr., brother, Dennis and sister-in-law, Leslie, my mother-in-law, Ms. Ann and extended family, Rev. Walter and Marjorie Kimbrough, Bobby and Sarah Lundy, Antonio and Gloria London, Cedric and Nicole Smith, Harry and Nino Colon, and Brett and Loni Perriman, Jenell Clark, Christine Nixon, LaShawn McConnell, Deborah Thomas, Beverly Smith, Thelma Day, and Cynthia Boyd, your support help me to enjoy a full life.

For my publisher, Moody/Lift Every Voice, and especially Greg Thornton, your belief in me helps me enjoy a career in writing.

For my 9th grade friends, Veida Evans, Kimberly Brickhouse Monroe, Jan Hatchett, and Vickie Randall Davis, your enduring friendship helps me enjoy my great past.

For my assistants on this series, Ciara Roundtree, Alyx Pinkston, Chantel Morgan, and Ashely Cheatum, your hard work helps me to enjoy the writing process.

For my children, Dustyn Leon, Sydni Derek, and Sheldyn Ashli, your reliance on me helps me to enjoy being your mom.

For my husband, Derrick Moore, your love helps me to enjoy each day.

For my readers, in particular those who don't have an easy life, your wounded souls help me to enjoy writing words that I pray will heal your hearts.

And for my precious Savior, who shields me from all harm, Your image helps me to enjoy who You created me to be.

# Discussion
## Questions

1. Yasmin Peace's parents announce they are moving. Do you feel the kids have a right to be upset about the move? What are some positive ways to deal with decisions your parents make that you don't agree with?

2. Yasmin is babysitting and the kids' real mom comes by for an unannounced visit. Do you think Yasmin was correct in letting her visit with the kids? When you are given strict guidelines from your parents, is there ever a time to break the rules?

3. Asia and Perlicia are now going out with Yasmin's brothers behind her back. Do you believe they were right in keeping this information from their friend? What lines in your friendships do you not want crossed?

4. Veida finds out that Asia and Perlicia now like York and Yancy. Do you feel Veida has a right to be angry, especially at Yasmin? What would you do if a friend got mad at you about something that was not your fault?

5. Yasmin goes to the Valentine's dance and runs into the new guy at the school. Do you think she should have let him hug her? What are healthy ways to grow new friendships?

6. Yasmin's mom loses her job. Do you think the kids are responsible to help her pay the bills? What are things you can do to help ease your parents' stress?

7. The landlord tells the family they are getting evicted. Do you think their mom is being prideful to not want help? When is accepting a helping hand not just taking a handout?

8. Yasmin and Veida are home alone until Asia and Perlica come over drunk. Do you think Yasmin should have let her intoxicated friends in? Is it okay to help a friend when you may get yourself in trouble in the process?

9. Yasmin sees Myrek, York, and Yancy being tempted to try drugs. Do you feel Yasmin is smart to butt in? What is another way to keep others out of trouble without getting directly involved?

10. Every time Yasmin goes to church she feels closer to God. Do you think she should go to church more often? Why do you think being connected in church is important?

11. Uncle John and Aunt Lucinda are sad they have to give the kids back. Do you think Uncle John is right in trusting God even when odds are not in his favor? Explain why you turn to God when things don't look good in your life.

12. Yasmin's parents get remarried, they don't have to move, and Uncle John and Aunt Lucinda get full custody of all three kids. What do you think the Peace family learned over the last two years? Explain the scripture Matthew 11:28–29 "Come unto me, all ye that labour and are heavy laden, and I will give you rest. Take my yoke upon you, and learn of me; for I am meek and lowly in heart: and ye shall find rest unto your souls."

# Finding Your Faith

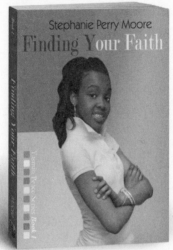

ISBN-13: 978-0-8024-8602-8

Yasmin Peace is growing up fast. After the tragic suicide of her oldest brother; she takes on the responsibility of overseeing what's left of her family and through it all; she perseveres. As she sheds her tomboy exterior and finds her faith, Yasmin blossoms into the young lady God destined her to become.

L E V B
LIFT EVERY VOICE BOOKS

LiftEveryVoiceBooks.com
MoodyPublishers.com

# Believing in Hope

ISBN-13: 978-0-8024-8603-5

In this second book of the Yasmin Peace series, family tensions and school unrest soar to a fever pitch. A school counselor begins the LIGHT club, a club dedicated to helping eighth grade girls deal with issues like gangs, depression, teen suicide, and self esteem. Yasmin discovers that there is hope on the other side of every obstacle— if she holds on to her faith.

**L E V B**
LIFT EVERY VOICE BOOKS

LiftEveryVoiceBooks.com
MoodyPublishers.com

# Experiencing the Joy

ISBN-13: 978-0-8024-8604-2

Graduating from eighth grade Yasmin starts summer on a positive note. Everything she's learned about self-esteem and true joy from the LIGHT club however will be put to the test as she faces new challenges with family, friends, and her first year in high school. Through it all Yasmin manages to hold on to hope and experience true joy.

L E V B
LIFT EVERY VOICE BOOKS
LiftEveryVoiceBooks.com
MoodyPublishers.com

# Learning to Love

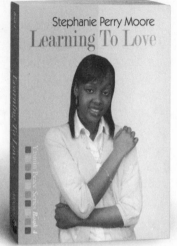

ISBN-13: 978-0-8024-8605-9

Yasmin Peace has been through a lot in the last year. After losing her oldest brother, Yasmin and her family lose their apartment in a fire. As if that was not enough Yasmin's grandmother is diagnosed with Alzheimer's. Through all of these difficult situations, Yasmin maintains hope. As she heads off to high school, things finally start to look up. She has three great friends, her father is out of jail and finally, all the drama is behind her. At least that's what Yasmin thinks. She has yet to learn the lessons of love as she finds out that loving those who are the closest to her is not always an easy thing to do.

L E V B
LIFT EVERY VOICE BOOKS

**LiftEveryVoiceBooks.com**
MoodyPublishers.com

# Lift Every Voice Books

Lift every voice and sing
Till earth and heaven ring,
Ring with the harmonies of Liberty;
Let our rejoicing rise
High as the listening skies,
Let it resound loud as the rolling sea.
Sing a song full of the faith that the dark past has taught us,
Sing a song full of the hope that the present has brought us,
Facing the rising sun of our new day begun
Let us march on till victory is won.

The Black National Anthem, written by James Weldon Johnson in 1900, captures the essence of Lift Every Voice Books. Lift Every Voice Books is an imprint of Moody Publishers that celebrates a rich culture and great heritage of faith, based on the foundation of eternal truth—God's Word. We endeavor to restore the fabric of the African-American soul and reclaim the indomitable spirit that kept our forefathers true to God in spite of insurmountable odds.

We are Lift Every Voice Books—Christ-centered books and resources for restoring the African-American soul.

For more information on other books and products
written and produced from a biblical perspective, go to
www.lifteveryvoicebooks.com or write to:

Lift Every Voice Books
820 N. LaSalle Boulevard
Chicago, IL 60610
www.LiftEveryVoiceBooks.com

WOODLAND HIGH SCHOOL
800 N. MOSELEY DRIVE
STOCKBRIDGE, GA 30281
(770) 389-2784